THE

AFTERMATH

ISBN Softcover 978-0-473-57838-1
ISBN ePub 978-1-991299-16-1

Cover art used with permission

Cataloguing in Publishing Data:

Title: The Aftermath

Author: Ricardo Camino

Subjects: New Zealand fiction, Apocalyptic thriller, Christian faith

A copy of this title is held at the National Library of New Zealand.

THE
AFTERMATH

Ricardo Camino

To Jade

CHARACTERS

Akira	-	Japanese cook
Ari	-	Man lost on road trip to Auckland
Caleb and Rhona	-	Missionaries from Keri Keri
Captain Burton-Smith	-	Captain of the Antarctica Princess
Captain Mori	-	Captain of Japanese Whaler
Cardiac Porter	-	Waitak Council Chairman
Carla	-	Aid post Medico at Waitak
Carson	-	Australian soldier shot in N.Z.
Chippy	-	Carpenter at Waitak
Colonel Petersen	-	Australian Army Officer
Compton & Marguerite Kingsford-Allen	-	Owners of Unitell, USA
Costello	-	Butcher, helicopter pilot at Waitak (dec.)
Flip	-	Youth from Taranaki
Gisborne (Giz) Jones	-	Security person at Waitak
Horse	-	Hairdresser at Waitak
J.B.	-	Security person
Kelly	-	Radio man, electrician

Mihi	-	Daughter of Spider, wife of Rick Carter
Quincy & Nancy	-	Quartermasters
Rick Carter	-	Shipwrecked Aussie
Spider	-	Church leader, Headmaster, Mihi's father
Thomas Draper	-	Spy and exile
Trueson	-	Spokesman for the Taranaki group
Ulysses & MariJayne Marchant	-	Owners of the All-American Digital TV Network
Watson	-	Mechanic at Waitak

CHAPTER ONE

Exhausted to the point of physical and mental numbness, Rick Carter crawled from the pounding surf on his hands and knees and collapsed face-down, head on forearms, in a line of spume and rotting seaweed. He was safe at last. Or so he thought.

For three unrelenting days and nights, Rick had battled the Easter cyclone that drove his small yacht south-eastwards, down the Tasman Sea. At the point of giving up, his vessel had grounded on a sandbank near the North Island's Manukau Heads. Deciding that the time had come to part company with his sinking boat, Rick unclipped his safety line and let the cresting rollers wash him ashore on a small bay at Whatipu. He was relieved to be on solid ground, even though it was New Zealand.

As his strength slowly returned, he recalled the ill-fated 'New Zealand Experiment.'

Twenty-eight years ago, a Dunedin laboratory had created an 'opossum-specific' disease to exterminate the seventy million Australian brushtail possums that were destroying the New Zealand endemic bush and bird life. It was a gratifying success, and New Zealand's expertise in genetic engineering was applauded world-wide. But a Waikato farmer's dog that had eaten a dying possum developed an aberrant strain of this pulmonary haemorrhagic disease which spread rapidly to other dogs, and from them to people. Not since the Spanish 'flu pandemic of 1918-19 which killed more than twenty-four million people world-wide, had humanity faced such a virulent and devastating disease. It robbed people of life within two weeks of experiencing their first symptoms. This rampant plague swept across Aotearoa New Zealand like a tidal wave, and in one month alone—the month of August—the population was decimated by this silent killer.

So swift and deadly was this 'Leoenzide epidemic'—as it was named by the overseas media—the country's seaports and airports were immediately closed, trapping many overseas visitors and business-people in the Land of the Long Black Cloud.

Like a gangrenous limb, New Zealand was cut off from the rest of the world. It was either that, or risk having this horrific plague become a pandemic that would spread its terrifying contagion all around the globe.

Large-scale attempts by the Australian authorities to help poison the wild dogs that still carried this disease had been only partly successful. Things quickly stalled when a helicopter based on an offshore aircraft carrier crashed after its bait-spreader snagged an unseen cable suspended across a deep road cutting. There was only one survivor, but before he could be rescued, wild dogs, apparently attracted by the smell of blood, attacked and mauled him. As a precaution, both the injured man and the rescue crew were kept in isolation. When they all died traumatic deaths, further flights over the country were called off.

Well, here was Rick in New Zealand, and his boat was filling with water out on a sandbar. While he had never visited the country before, his father had flown to Auckland for an America's Cup race. Back then, Auckland was called 'the City of Sails,' and Rick remembered from his father's photos the large marinas with their parked-up yachts in Auckland's Waitemata Harbour.

If he was to get away from this country and back to Australia, he had to do it all by himself. He decided that his immediate goal would be to get himself over land to Auckland's Harbour, where he hoped to find a suitable ocean-going yacht that he could sail single-handedly back across the Tasman.

Struggling to his feet, Rick could make out, through the steady downpour, some cottages nestled up against the hills only a short distance from the beach. Inside one of them, he removed his life-jacket and sodden clothing and dried himself down with a moth-eaten bedspread before stretching out on a bare mattress and falling instantly asleep.

About mid-morning the next day, Rick awoke with a dry mouth. After quenching his thirst at a small nearby stream, he set about searching the buildings for food. The floors and furniture throughout were covered with a layer of fine sand, disturbed only by the footprints of mice. He found some canned food in the larger of the buildings but the tins were rusty and swollen. In the storeroom, however, he discovered some rice in a sealed glass jar. It looked and smelled reasonably good.

As the skies were clearing, Rick crushed some wooden chairs into kindling and lit a fire outdoors on which to cook some of the rice, using a saucepan from the kitchen. Remembering his mother's mantra, he added two cups of water and a pinch of salt to one cup of rice, and brought it to the boil. After eating his fill, he poured what was left of the uncooked rice into a container and set out on foot along what remained of the road that went up over the hill, away from the beach.

The margins of the bush on either side of the road were closing in, leaving only a narrow track which, in places, had been deeply scoured by water. Dips in the road, where leaf litter had collected and decomposed, were now clothed in thickets of manuka, making progress slow. The afternoon was well advanced by the time he reached the tiny village of Little Huia overlooking the Manukau Harbour. In the garden shed of one of the houses at the water's edge, he found a fishing line and decided to try his hand at catching something appetising for tea. With his knife he lifted a small shellfish from a rock and threaded its meat onto a fish hook. After a satisfying meal of fish and boiled rice, he settled down in the best of the beachside houses for the night.

The next morning, Rick was up with the birds. He ate what remained of the previous evening's meal and then set out for a larger settlement he could see further up the bay. At the entrance to the village of Huia, he picked his way across a broken, curved concrete bridge that appeared to have been shattered by a large earthquake. In a garage at the top of a steep drive, he found an ancient Austin 6 sedan that someone had lovingly restored.

Fortunately, this car was sitting on blocks, so its tyres were still in reasonable shape. They needed only extra air, which he forced into the inner tubes with a foot pump that he found under a bench at the rear of the garage.

This antique car had a crank handle rather than a starter motor. After syphoning condensation from the fuel tank, Rick got its engine started with the help of a magneto that he removed from an old Case tractor. The sweet sound of the idling engine made his heart leap with excitement.

Early the following day, Rick set out for Auckland, anticipating that he would get there before nightfall. He came across his first major obstacle at the base of a hill near a beach. The road went down a steep slope, crossed a bridge, and continued up an equally steep slope on the other side. He could see that the deep drains that flanked the road on both sides of the bridge had blocked up at the bottoms many years ago, with the result that the sturdy concrete bridge across the creek had about a metre of sand and silt deposited on it. Scores of shrubs and trees, some of them up to four metres high, were growing in an impenetrable thicket from one end of the bridge to the other. And across the front edge of this green barrier grew several bulrushes and a couple of large flax plants.

Rick got out of the car to have a look round. He figured that with an axe and a spade he could clear a track on the southern side, wide enough for the car to get through.

On his return from Huia with the necessary tools he started chopping and digging. He had almost finished when he heard dogs snarling and barking down on the beach. Moving to where he could see through the trees, he counted a pack of nine large but otherwise non-descript animals on the shore. They were fighting over what appeared to be the carcass of a fur-seal pup. Not wanting to be discovered, he returned to the car and shut himself inside, winding the windows up to minimise the chance of his scent reaching them. Rick was still cooped up inside the car an hour later when it started to rain again in a steady downpour.

Water coursed down the hill ahead and swept across the road beneath the car, piling up debris around the wheels. The last thing he wanted was to attract the attention of the dogs, so he stayed put. As the day wore on, he realised he would be there for the night so made himself as comfortable as possible in his rather cold and cramped quarters.

Sometime after midnight, Rick became aware of movement and sniffing outside. A large, mangy brown dog with a torn ear stood up on its hind legs and raked his side-window with its forepaws. Rick banged on the glass with his fist. In response the dog curled its top lip and showed its teeth in a snarl. In the dim light of the moon Rick noted that the pack of dogs ranging around his vehicle and urinating on the wheels was not the same pack he had seen earlier down on the beach. As the car could only be started with a crank handle, it occurred to him that he would be trapped inside until the animals departed.

A short time later, his thoughts were interrupted by fierce dogfight that exploded in the darkness. By the number of dogs involved, Rick guessed the local pack had come upon the intruders and were intent on driving them out of their territory. The fight went on for fifteen or more minutes, and gradually moved further and further away. Then and there, Rick decided that he had to find himself a gun and some ammunition to improve his chances of survival.

Next morning, with a rumbling stomach reminding him that he hadn't eaten for several hours, Rick finished the track across the bridge and got the car through to the road on the other side. Expecting to be over the Waitakere range and into Auckland in no time at all, he drove along with the window down, singing 'Waltzing Matilda' at the top of his voice. About fifteen minutes later he came to the base of a large water reservoir up on the left side of the road. As he got closer, he could see that the concrete road bridge over the deep overflow channel that ran from the reservoir down to the beach, had collapsed—further evidence of a large earthquake. There was no way around so there was no alternative but to continue his journey on foot until he could find some other means of transport. As he was getting out of the car, he thought he heard a rifle shot echoing around the hills. He stood there for a while listening and wondering, but hearing nothing further he shrugged his shoulders, climbed down into the channel, picked his way over the broken concrete of the shattered bridge at the bottom, and hoisted himself up and out the other side.

Suddenly, Rick was startled by the sound of a couple of dogs snapping at each other just around the bend ahead. In a panic, he turned and sprinted up a short side-road on his left. Near the road's end he stopped, hands on knees, gasping for breath. When he stood up, there in front of him was a lichen-covered sign with the words "Pipeline Walk" barely readable. On the other side of a rusty steel gate, he found an all-weather road, with a large pipe on the upper side running through a tunnel of bush. Apparently, this was the water pipe that ran from the nearby reservoir to the city. He followed it, walking quickly, trying to put as much distance as possible between himself and the dogs, should they pick up his scent.

Part-way along this path, Rick came to another gate. Beyond it, he could see a sealed road and some over-grown houses. He hoped that in one of them he might find some kind of weapon with which he could defend himself; preferably a loaded shot-gun or rifle. The tree-shaded exteriors of these houses were green with moss and algae, and vines covered their paint-pealed walls and roofs. Numerous shrubs grew in the valleys of the roofs. The rainwater spouting had, in many places, been ripped away by the sheer weight of the mass of plants growing in the decomposing leaf litter that filled them. Where there were once neat lawns and gardens were now thickets of black wattle, privet and coprosma.

There was no suitable weapon in the first house, as far as he could see, because the rooms were dark, there being no electricity for lighting. Wanting to quench his thirst, he tried the tap at the kitchen sink, but there was no running water either.

On his way to the next house, he disturbed a large sow with eight to ten piglets foraging in a thicket of bushes. The sight of a fat young piglet near the steps to the back door accentuated Rick's hunger pains. He calculated that he could grab it and get inside the house before the sow, who was now watching him and grunting for her litter, could get to him. He badly underestimated the speed of the sow, however, for he had scarcely grabbed the squealing suckling when she took his legs from under him and dropped him onto his back. The sow and the piglet escaped into the bush, but just then, from the rear of the property, came the sound of splintering sticks.

Rick looked over his shoulder to see a long-snouted boar with wicked tusks thrusting its way through the thicket towards him. Springing to his feet, Rick tugged a stout garden stake out of the ground, raised it over his shoulder and, with all his might, swung it down so that its narrow edge struck the advancing boar across his snout. The angry animal, squealing loudly with fury and pain, lowered his head and charged his assailant.

Deciding that retreat was now better than valour, Rick turned and sprinted out onto the road, looking left and right for a way of escape. Up ahead there was a tree with a low branch that he could reach in a leap.

The following events were a confused blur. Either Rick tripped, or the boar had caught hold of his foot. In any case, Rick fell forward and the furious boar was upon him instantly, slicing through his trousers and into his left buttock with a razor-sharp tusk. Rick instinctively curled into a foetal position to protect his stomach, covering his head with his arms, expecting the worst.

The crack of a gun nearby turned the table and the Captain Cooker spun around, trembled and fell across Rick's shoulder and neck, pulsing blood over him. Pushing the convulsing pig off with one hand and pressing on his torn buttock with the other, Rick staggered to his feet and looked around. An attractive Maori woman in her mid-twenties came toward him with a semi-automatic in her right hand. "Kia ora," she said with a smile. "I'm Mihi. I don't believe we've met."

CHAPTER TWO

R ick stood there with his mouth open, totally at a loss for words. He was thankful for this woman's intervention, but where on earth had she come from?

Noticing blood seeping through the fingers that Rick was pressing against his incised buttock, Mihi grimaced. "Ooo!" she exclaimed, "That's a nasty wound you've got there! I'll need to wash it out with some disinfectant and put a temporary dressing on it to staunch the bleeding until it can be treated properly."

Mihi ran diagonally across the road and went up a drive on the other side. Although in considerable pain, Rick couldn't help but notice how gracefully this lithe and stunning woman moved. A few moments later he heard a motor start, and saw her come back on a quad bike towing a small galvanised steel trailer.

Opening the toolbox on the trailer, she took out a red first aid kit. As she gently washed out his wound with disinfectant, Rick said, "I thought I was the only person alive in this country. How did you get here?"

"Oh, I was born here, and I've lived here all my life. How did you get here?"

"I was ship-wrecked on the west coast," he replied. "The storm that uprooted some of these trees here would have been the same one that blew me down through the Tasman Sea and landed me ashore at Whatipu."

"Whereabouts at Whatipu?"

"Not far from a pointy rock with a small lighthouse on it."

"Yes, I know the place. Where were you when the storm first caught you?" she asked as she taped a wad of material to his wound.

"I was sailing down the Great Barrier Reef. The cyclone wasn't supposed to come my way, but it changed direction quickly and caught me."

"But wait!" exclaimed Rick, changing the subject, "the rest of the world has been led to believe that the disease, Leoenzide, wiped out everyone in this country. How come it didn't kill you?"

"It's too long a story to start now," Mihi said. "I'll tell you later. Give me your shirt, please." She took Rick's bloodied shirt and left.

When she returned with the shirt, it was clean but wet.

"Think you can get yourself onto the pillion seat?" Mihi asked, nodding her head towards the quad bike. "We've got a way to go."

Rick gingerly climbed aboard while she expertly gutted the pig with her sheath knife and then, with knees bent, swung the porker's carcass up onto the trailer with a fluid motion. In one corner of the trailer Rick could see a large native pigeon with its head shot off.

A little further up the road, just before a high steel transmission mast on a hill, Mihi turned off into what was once a very smart home.

She eased him off the bike, then parked it in the garage. Rick's leg was now stiffening up and becoming quite painful. Mihi put her arm around his waist and helped him limp into the house.

"Excuse the pun," said Rick, "but thanks for saving my bacon."

"Make yourself as comfortable as possible," she said as she took a walkie-talkie from a pouch on her belt, and went back outside. "We'll be here for some time," she added on her way out.

Rick could hear the low murmur of her voice but couldn't pick up anything she was saying. He guessed that her walkie-talkie wouldn't have a very great range, which meant there must be at least one other person within a few kilometres.

When Mihi came back inside, Rick said, "I've been looking at your gun. It's Indonesian."

"You know guns?"

"No. I've never owned one. I lived in Jakarta for two years and I recognised the manufacturer's name. How did you come by it?"

"Eight years ago, when the main road to the East Coast was still usable, a couple of men went over to Tauranga on a recce."

"How many are there of you?" Rick asked. Mihi ignored his question and continued:

"From up in the hills they could see a tent encampment down on a grassy field in a park not far from the waterfront. A flagpole there had a limp red and white Indonesian flag hanging from it. The men stayed up in the hills for two days, watching through binoculars, but seeing no movement at all they moved cautiously down towards the encampment.

"It appeared to them that the Indonesians had come to re-colonise our country, but had become infected by the Leoenzide virus themselves, so had set up a field hospital in the park to care for their sick and dying. There were skeletons in rags in every tent. Scores of them. They had been dead a long time. This gun was a part of the cache of weapons belonging to the military personnel sent here to assist and protect the new immigrants. The weapons were lighter and more high-tech than what we had. And as there were several cases of ammunition with them, we adopted them."

Rick had so much more that he wanted to ask Mihi, but she insisted that he tell her about himself. So, for the next twenty minutes, he answered questions about where he had come from, the places he had lived and worked in, the kind of work he was now engaged in, his family relationships, his hobbies, his personal values and beliefs. The conversation was interrupted by the sound of a quad bike approaching from the north. It stopped outside. The door opened and a young part-Polynesian, part-European woman entered. She, also, was toting an Indonesian semi-automatic. Mihi stood up and said, "Ricky, this is Carla. Carla, Ricky."

Carla nodded and smiled faintly as she took a small rucksack off her back, opened it, and removed a plastic container and a pair of jeans.

"These should fit you," she said, passing them to Rick. "When did you last have a tetanus shot?" she asked as she levered the lid off the container.

"Ah, about two years ago."

"Good. I'll clean your wound, apply a topical anaesthetic, and suture it up."

After she had covered the stitched muscle with plaster, she opened two small brown bottles and shook some tablets onto her hand. "I want you to take these," she said.

"What are they for? Rick asked.

"These two are oral pain killers," she said, pointing to the two white tablets. "The light brown lozenge is a very effective antidote to the deadly virus carried by wild dogs. It'll give you a head start should you come in contact with it in the next few days."

Rick swallowed the tablets with the aid of a swig from her water bottle.

Mihi said, "I have something I need to attend to for a while outside so, if you don't mind, I'll leave you two to entertain each other until I get back."

After Mihi had gone, Carla turned to Rick and said, "I'd love to hear how you ended up here in Aotearoa."

"You should have been here earlier," replied Rick, "I've just shared my life-story with Mihi."

"Never mind. I'm sure you won't mind telling me too. You're the first visitor we've had for a long, long time, so I'm keen to hear anything and everything you can tell me about the outside world."

And so, prompted by Carla's questions, Rick retold the story of his life in Port Douglas through to the foundering of his yacht, *SpinDrift*, at the Manukau Heads. He had barely finished when, as if on cue, Mihi returned. Both women went outside, and he could hear them conferring. When they returned and asked him to clarify certain things, he realised that they had been comparing the two accounts he had given, and that their earlier casual questioning had actually been subtle third-degree investigations.

After double-checking some minor issues in his account, Mihi said they would need to keep him under observation at the house for a couple of nights. He could leave if he wished, but if he did so he would be on his own.

Rick told them that he chose to stay; in his present state he didn't really have much choice. They asked him what his reading preferences were. He said he would like a book of New Zealand maps, plus a good crime or thriller novel.

Some time later, Rick heard a motorbike with a very throaty exhaust-pipe approaching from the north. When it arrived, Mihi went outside and Carla moved to the kitchen. Rick could hear Mihi talking with someone so he hopped over to a window and saw her engaged in a conversation with two well-built young men. One of them took Mihi's quad bike and trailer with the porker and pigeon in it and drove off. The other left in the opposite direction on his cross-country bike.

Time at the house passed quickly, with Carla and Mihi doing alternate shifts so as to be able to tend to Rick's needs at all times. They encouraged Rick to go for short walks to improve the circulation to his wound, but asked him not to go more than ten minutes from the house. When he asked about the possibility of running into wild dogs, they told him that the dogs in the immediate area had been exterminated and that those on the perimeters had been shot at so many times they avoided contact with people.

Whenever Rick tried to engage either of the women in conversation, they avoided his questions and would only talk in generalities. Eventually he gave up, and either slept or read his novel.

About noon on Tuesday, there was the welcome sound of a cross-country bike approaching. It stopped outside the front door and one of the young men, whom Rick had seen earlier through the window, came into the house holding a water-damaged book with a black cover that looked strangely familiar. "Kia ora, J.B.," greeted Mihi. "Did you have any success?"

J.B. opened the book and laid it on the table. "That's my log book!" Rick exclaimed as he moved to the table to get a closer look. "Where did you get that?"

"I went out to your boat. By the way, they call me J.B.," he said offering his hand.

"Rick," responded Rick, returning the firm grip.

"Thanks for the track you cut through the bush on the bridge. You have made it much easier to get across that stream," he smiled.

"My pleasure," replied Rick.

"Rick, we had to be sure that you are who you said you were," continued J.B. "That's why it was necessary for us to check out your story. We were tricked once before, and several people were killed as a result."

"People killed? How? What happened?"

"If you don't mind, Rick, I'd like something to eat before I answer your questions. I haven't had a decent meal for a while and I'm starving."

Carla and Mihi served up a tasty lunch for everyone, and while they ate, J.B. answered Rick's question. "Ten years ago, a man, who called himself Thomas Draper, claimed, as you did, to have lost his boat off-shore. We believed him and took him to our settlement."

Rick's mind grappled with these new facts. A settlement meant that there were more people.

"The very next day," J.B. continued, "Draper acted strangely when Costello came upon him rather suddenly. Draper, who was studying something in his hand, very guiltily stuffed it into his pocket. Costello pretended that he hadn't noticed and struck up a casual conversation with him. Afterwards, Costello went to the Chairman of the Council and reported his suspicions. That night they prepared a hot bath for the visitor, and while he was luxuriating in the soapy water, we searched his gear. He didn't have much so it didn't take us long to find a small GPS tracker, and a mini R.T. (Radio Transceiver), both in secret pockets set into the flotation material of his lifejacket. These concealments made us rather apprehensive. We said nothing, but from that moment on we kept him under a twenty-four-hour watch.

"The very next morning, at four-thirty, Draper sneaked out of the village and climbed a big hill about a kilometre away. I had been appointed to keep an eye on him during that watch, so I shadowed him. Near the crest of the hill, I could hear him talking on his R.T. As I moved closer, I heard him give the GPS co-ordinates for our village to the person he was talking to. He said that he himself was away from the village and it was now over to them.

"It took me a few moments to cotton on to what was going on, but when it dawned on me, I raced back to the village as fast as my legs would carry me. Just on the outskirts I could hear jet aircraft flying in from the west coast. I rushed in among the houses yelling at the top of my voice, and with a steel bar banged the empty gas cylinder that we had hanging from a tree branch, 'Get out! Get out everyone! Run! Run for your lives! Get up into the bush!'

"Two aircraft circled around to make a run down our valley and came in low, one following the other, dumping a rolling wave of flaming napalm on our settlement. Three adults and two children never made it. Some, among those who escaped, received first and second-degree burns. It was awful. One day, if you would like, we will take you to see the place."

"How come we never heard anything about this in Australia?" Rick asked incredulously. "We have been told that there are absolutely no people alive at all in this country, so why on earth would they want to kill you? It doesn't make sense."

"They probably believe that we are carriers of the disease and are afraid that we might try to get to Australia," continued J.B. "Fear does strange things to people. Remember the Covid 19 pandemic? The same reasoning may be driving their reaction to Leoenzide."

"Have any of you ever tried to get to Australia?"

"Yes. We've made two attempts to get to the outside world with the truth about our situation here but it seems our boats never made it. We suspect that they are watching us all the time. A submarine has been seen on several occasions, and there are daily aerial patrols along both coastlines."

"Are you carriers of the disease?"

"Of course not! If anyone got it, they didn't survive more than a week or so. The late Doc. Smithers observed that nearly everyone who had been taking Avatrox, an oral antibiotic, recovered from the plague's deadly side-effects, so we raided all the pharmacies, and now we have a good stock of Avatrox on-hand in a controlled environment. In the early days, however, the plague decimated the population, and we have good reason to believe that wild dogs are still carriers that could infect people who are not protected by Avatrox."

"What happened to Draper?"

"Early next morning we found his radio transceiver. It appears that he had got tangled in some barbed lawyer vine and had fallen down a bank where he dropped it. But because of the terrain and the undergrowth in that place he was unable to find it again. We sent out a search party to bring him in."

"That story really disturbs me," said Rick thoughtfully. "I find it hard to believe that the Australian navy would have done that to you." After a pause Rick continued, "How did your community survive after having its homes burned up?"

"As soon as it was daylight, we took everyone to our gardens in the next valley where there was food, water and limited shelter. Later, four men were detailed to return and bury the remains of the folk who were napalmed. They had only just entered the clearing when they heard a chopper coming, so moved back into the bush. We think the chopper had come to collect Draper, because after it landed, the three crew members just got out and stood under a nearby tree waiting.

"Smiley, whose wife had been killed in the napalm dump, was one of those detailed to bury the dead. He lost his cool, stepped out into the open and called, "Good morning gentlemen!" When they turned around, he shot them: *Bang! bang! bang!* The others berated him for his stupidity, because when the chopper didn't return to the carrier, they would come looking for it. Our folk were saved, however, by a pack of wild dogs that had been attracted by the smell of scorched flesh, so our guys retreated and left the animals to it. By the time the dogs had finished there was nothing left but shreds of clothing and splinters of bone.

"Towards sunset another chopper arrived. It landed beside the one on the ground. The crew got out, took photos, collected all that remained of the dead men and the remnants of their clothing, and departed. They had brought a second pilot and both choppers returned to the aircraft carrier."

"You didn't say whether you caught Draper."

"Yes, we captured him. Some wanted to shoot him, but our court decided to exile him to the Coromandel with the threat that if he was ever seen in our area again, he would be shot on sight. We have no idea whether he is still alive or not. The same court also tried Smiley for killing the helicopter crew. He was given a year's detention for each death. During that three-year period, he had to work three days a week in the communal gardens and wasn't permitted to attend any of the social gatherings or have any interaction with the opposite gender. On appeal that sentence was reduced to eighteen months as he was grieving the loss of his own wife."

"Even so, that was a pretty tough sentence!"

"Not really. Those men he killed had families they wouldn't be going home to."

"But they were out to kill you."

"We are not responsible for what they do to us. We are, however, responsible for what we do to them. But let's talk later. We should to be on our way. Mihi will take you on her bike."

CHAPTER THREE

Rick climbed stiffly onto the pillion seat and the three bikes set off along the road to the north, travelling about fifty metres apart. When they came to a stop, J.B. dismounted and reached through some coprosmas growing on the left side of the road, unlocked and swung back a wall of shrubs to reveal a sealed road going down the ridge on the other side. On closer inspection, Rick could see that the shrubs were growing in a stainless-steel trough on the inside of a heavy, camouflage green galvanised-pipe gate. The shrubs and vines had grown around and through the gate in such a manner that the gate itself was invisible from the main road, making it look like a continuation of the roadside bush.

They moved through and after shutting and locking the gate behind them, drove down a steep sealed driveway to a house at the bottom, near a large water reservoir. They parked their bikes in a garage there and helped Rick down a flight of concrete steps on the face of the concrete dam wall to a narrow-gauge railway that ran back along one side of the steep valley. At the bottom of the steps, they mounted a jigger and pumped it along the rails to some small, neat cabins with shingle roofs set back in the trees. Each of these cabins was painted in shades of green and brown that blended in with the surrounding bush.

Men, women and children were standing in a small paved square. They had heard that Rick was coming and were curious to see the newcomer. The kiddies smiled shyly and waved tentatively to him. That made him feel more at ease. He smiled and waved back.

Mihi said, "We'll save introductions until tea time. Come with me." She helped Rick up a sloping path to a cabin built among the trees. "This is your temporary home," she said. "You will be living with Horse until you choose your own accommodation."

"Living with who?" Rick asked with a part smile.

"With Horse," said Mihi. "He's a neat guy. You'll like him. He's our hairdresser"

"Why is he called Horse?"

"You'll find out soon enough," Mihi said with a laugh.

She banged on the door and a huge, rugged man with a large bushy beard, a barrel-like chest and a twinkle in his eyes, swung the door inwards and filled the opening.

"Horse, this is Rick. He will be staying with you for a while."

Horse came down the steps with his hand outstretched on a rigid arm.

"Pleased to meet you, Horse," he said.

"He calls everyone Horse," laughed Mihi over her shoulder as she departed.

That evening, at a specially organised outdoor communal tea, Rick was introduced to seventy-four people who ranged in age from the very old to the very young. Mihi told him that there were four others who were absent.

The first thing Rick noticed was that there wasn't a single obese person among them. The main course that evening featured the wild boar that Mihi had shot. Before the meal started, Cardiac Porter, the Chairman of the Council, presented Rick with the tusks that one of the settlement's artisans had removed from the boar and mounted on a small shield of pale waxed puriri wood.

Stepping to the front, Cardiac clapped his hands to call everyone to attention. "When people come to each other's aid in a time of crisis, the bonds that are formed are always very special. On behalf of the Waitak community, I present these mounted tusks to you, Mr. Carter, as a token of the crisis that brought us together, and of the support that we pledge to offer you as long as you are with us. It is a rare privilege to be able to welcome a new person into our iwi and, with your permission, we would like to adopt you as a member of our community."

"Thank you sincerely," Rick replied as he stood up, leaning on Horse's shoulder. "I am in debt to you for my life. I appreciate your willingness to accept me as a part of your extended family. I want to assert, however, that I will remain here only until I can find a way to get back to Australia. In the meantime, I shall willingly carry my weight in this community and submit myself to its rules and regulations. I especially want to thank the beautiful maiden, Mihi, for saving my life. I owe my survival to her skill and coolness." Everyone clapped, and Rick was mobbed by people wanting to talk with him.

That night he and Horse lay on their bunks and talked till the wee hours of the morning. "You are a strange bunch," said Rick into the darkness. "Your whole community goes against the grain."

"What do you mean?" asked Horse, suddenly alert.

"In a situation such as your group is in, life becomes a matter of the survival of the fittest. People are inclined to give away any ethics they ever had when they are answerable to no one. They become self-centred and bestial, fighting over land and women."

"Yeh. We were like that in the beginning," commented Horse.

"That's hard to believe! What changed you?"

"It's quite a story, horse. Mihi's mother was brutally raped by Spider. You met him tonight. He's the Maori man with the grey beard. Mihi is the child of that illicit liaison. The rapist was caught, and the community was going to lynch him right then and there. But his friend, Ari, pled that Spider be exiled instead. Nobody, however, was willing to give Spider the opportunity to return and kill them in their sleep, so most of us strongly opposed that suggestion. Then Ari—a man everyone trusted—said he would go with Spider and keep an eye on him. After a lot of discussion Ari's proposal was accepted.

"The two men decided to make find a suitable place to live up north. They set out on horseback, but on the way, they saw smoke just out of Whangarei and found a small group of people who were on their last legs. These folks had built a high fence around their compound to keep out the dogs, but in-fighting and fear in the group had taken its toll. When Ari told them about Avatrox, it was as if the sun had broken through the murk after a cyclone. Some recalled that they had been taking the drug at the time of the plague, and so had been protected. Anyway, ample supplies of Avatrox were found in the city's pharmacies, so they stocked up. It's a drug that still works after all these years. Well, Ari was a natural leader, and after a few days they decided to go with him to start a new colony further north in Keri Keri, where it would be warm enough to grow kumara, our sweet potato, and was close to a river and the sea, both good food sources.

"Now Spider, for all his faults, was an avid reader. He found a Bible and, having nothing else to read at the time, decided to give it a go. Slowly, a profound change came over this man. People would come across him weeping over its open pages. He would hurriedly wipe away the tears with his arm and make some lame excuse about wind-blown pollen in his eyes.

"One day, Spider began to teach one of the men to read and write. He did so well, others wanted him to do the same for them, so he got some materials together and started a class. It was a mixture of Bible teaching and general subjects. Soon the classes were catering to adults and children alike. Parents began to notice changes in their kids. They were happier, more obedient and more caring. Within six months practically the whole group was transformed. Then, one day, two and a half years after they had left the Auckland group, Ari decided the time had come for him to return home. Spider was a different man and no longer a threat to anyone. And he also had a supportive community around him. Ari's concern was now for the people back in Auckland. They were in an emotional mess through the trauma of the plague and the grief of losing their loved ones, and he was convinced that the Bible would help them, too. Well, for some unknown reason, Ari never got to Auckland. He just disappeared. Nobody ever found out what had happened to him. The Keri Keri group suspected that something had gone wrong when his messenger-pigeon returned to them without a message.

"Several months later two others, Caleb and Rhona, decided to make the journey to Auckland. Spider gave them directions to the community and a letter of introduction to the Council. The folk in Auckland were thrilled to hear that there was another group of survivors, but they weren't at all open to any talk about the Bible. Eventually Caleb and Rhona felt that the one person who would make a change for good in this deeply divided community would be Spider, himself. But how could they persuade the people to invite him back? They guessed that they would have only one chance to present their case to the Council so it would have to be good. From that time forward they made it their mission, whenever they went out with the community to work in the gardens, to spend time with Mihi's mother. Once they had become good friends, they shared with her the profound changes that had come into Spider's life, and the tears he had shed over what he had done. At first, she only sneered, but when she heard about the change that had come to the whole community, she began to listen and ask questions.

"Caleb and Rhona knew they were getting somewhere when Mihi's mother said to them one day, 'We could do with that kind of change here. We should be working together instead of tearing ourselves apart. The kids need education, and the adults need to wake up to what's happening to us all. Gambling is becoming a way of life, and drunken fights have become commonplace.' When Rhona said to Mihi's mum, 'I know only one person who could make that kind of change—Spider,' she exploded. The next day, however, she went to Rhona and apologised, saying, 'If Spider has become the kind of man you say he is, and if he can help us, then, perhaps, we should ask the Council to invite him to come back home.'

"Rhona said she didn't think the Council would invite him back on those grounds. They would be deeply suspicious of a rapist-turned-Bible-basher. A far better case would be for her to state that he had been in exile for four years, and that he was profoundly sorry for what he had done. Furthermore, she needed the father in the home to help bring up their daughter, Mihi. Would the Council please rescind its exile action and invite him home? There would be minimal risk as he had not only lived an upright life but had been responsible for transforming the Keri Keri community into a happy, successful unit with most people gainfully employed in a trade or business.

"The Council was in meeting all morning and loud voices were heard from time to time. Eventually a spokesperson came out to say that they had decided to permit Spider to return, but he would be on probation for six months. If there were any hint of trouble from him, he would be expelled again with no chance of ever returning.

"When Spider got back to Auckland he was greeted with silence and sullen looks. But he started right in with his mission. He didn't preach, but worked hard at gathering the materials that he needed and started a school. At first only a few attended, but within three months every kid was in attendance. No one lifted a finger to help him, though. He did it all by himself. But the people were watching. I tell you, Horse, they watched his every move. He ran morning classes for the kids and, later on, afternoon classes for the adults. His emphasis was on teaching life skills and life values, plus basic reading, writing and arithmetic. He seconded other people from the settlement to help teach subjects like the Maori language, horse care, leather work, carpentry, music, bee-keeping, cooking, health, and so on. And he also got together a lending-library of good books. After a time, a small church was started, and the people set aside every Saturday as their rest and worship day."

"Saturday? You mean Sunday, don't you?" interjected Rick.

"Nope! Spider said that Saturday was the customary day that Jesus and the apostles went to church and he couldn't find any record in the Bible of people going to church on Sunday as a regular thing. Besides, the fourth of the Ten Commandments says, "The seventh day is a Sabbath to the Lord your God." And the seventh day of the week has always been Saturday. Check it out in any dictionary or standard calendar.

"Spider asked Woody, a harmonica player, to get all the village musicians together and start a band. It's a motley group comprised of a drummer, a clarinet and a saxophone player, plus a violinist. The young folk who are learning to play recorders and guitars join the church musicians as they become more competent. There are two talented musicians who compose music and worship songs, and every Saturday morning there is a right royal jam session. You've never heard anything like it, Horse. After a twenty-minute Bible-based sermon, we all pray together, and for each other, and then share personal testimonies of what the Lord has done for us, or is doing in and through us. There have been a few baptisms as well, which have been great celebrations of a converted person's total submission and commitment to the Lord Jesus.

"As Spider won our confidence and support, he began to institute other changes. A monthly post was established between the Keri Keri and Auckland settlements. He then put forward the idea that the two groups get together for a three-day outing and social gathering at Port Albert—a small village on the Kaipara Harbour, about half way between the settlements. The whole Auckland group—men, women and children—travelled up a couple of days before the event to prepare the hall, accommodation and food. It was an exciting and refreshing break. Besides socialising, there were several meetings where people shared ideas and recipes, and other things. Many new friendships were made. One of our young ladies fell in love with a young man from Keri Keri, so a family from there took her in until they got married. And we have gained a couple of talented young women from their group. One is a post-primary teacher, and the other a horse trainer. Also, everybody agreed that the post riders do a fortnightly rather than monthly run so that they could keep in touch more frequently. That combined meeting has since been called the 'Salvation Convention.'"

"Why was that?"

"Because, Horse, both groups returned home to find their settlements totally destroyed and burnt. It appears that several helicopters had landed at both places simultaneously and that commandos had gone in with guns and flame- throwers to wipe out the people they believed were carriers of the plague. Not finding any people, they burnt down their dwellings. We were both devastated at the loss of our property and simultaneously full of praise that not a single person had been lost. We held a thanksgiving meeting right there in the ashes. I can tell you, Horse, that after that experience there were few doubters. Almost every last person became a disciple of Jesus. And every year since, we have gone back to that site on the anniversary of that occasion to hold a thanksgiving celebration and to share with our children what the Lord did for us back then.

"A decision was made to get away from the old village as quickly as possible. We moved out into the country where there was water and stayed there for six weeks while the men prepared housing for their families at the new site. We shifted to the new location and were there until Draper organised the second raid. After that, we moved to this site and, as you are discovering, we have taken extraordinary precautions to keep it secret. The only building with a steel roof is the one that was already here. It's the house where you parked the bikes. All other buildings, as you have seen, are erected beneath the trees. They are kept small, and are all roofed with wooden shingles. Underneath each cabin is a concrete cellar with a fireproof trap door. We have no open fires, but have a reliable hydroelectric system a bit further down the valley which is powered by water from the dam above. It provides electricity for cooking, lighting, heating and refrigeration. We have done our best to reduce heat loss from the cabins and school as the Australian spy planes that check us out every day probably have infrared detectors.

"Our people are nomadic during most of the week. We have a mini train that takes us through a tunnel right under the ridge that the main road runs along, out onto the flat land on the other side. It is out there that we have our brush-fenced gardens, deliberately kept small and scattered so that they will not be obvious to a spy plane."

"How do you know there are spy planes?"

"Every now and then we pick one up with our binoculars. They are difficult to detect as they fly so high and quietly, but we often pick one up when it flies beneath low cloud."

When Rick awoke the next day, the sun was already well up. Horse had a plate of baked kumara and pumpkin, together with steamed puha and half a roasted kereru breast on the table for him. "Eat up, Horse," he said. "We live on two meals a day here, one in the morning and another at the end of the day. If you want your leg to get better you need good food."

"You're not wrong there. I didn't eat anything during the cyclone, and haven't really had a balanced diet since."

"Listen," said Horse. "The people at this settlement, which we call Waitak, normally go out to their farms each Tuesday arvo. They stayed here yesterday in order to meet you and put on a welcome party for you. This morning, however, they will be moving off. But not all will go. Several of us will be staying behind. I'm telling you this so that you will understand when you notice that the place looks a little deserted."

Rick had just finished scraping his plate clean when Carla turned up to put a new dressing on his leg. She was saying how pleased she was that the wound looked so healthy, when Mihi arrived in bare feet. Her shiny black hair was tucked behind her left ear and Rick detected a lavender-like perfume. This was the first time he had really looked at her. Up till now the pain of his buttock wound had kept him rather self-absorbed. There was no doubt about it, she was all woman, full of grace and beauty. When Carla noticed the way he looked at her, she stiffened and gave a snort. "Morena Ricky," greeted Mihi with a big grin. "I've come to show you around our village. That's if you would like me to?"

"I'd like that very much," he replied.

"There's not a lot to show you," said Mihi as they stepped out. "We have sufficient homes for all our people, plus a store house, which includes an underground cool store. Over there is our school building, which also serves as our library, meeting place and church. And that is our medical dispensary, which is Carla's responsibility. We don't have enough land here for much else. Oh, yes, the house at the end of the road that has the garage where we left the bikes—it serves as our shop we can buy milk, yoghurt, jams and preserves, eggs, wild honey, raupo pollen cakes, cottage cheese, and pumpkin bread. All provided by our community."

"You've done a great deal with so little," said Ricky. "But why on earth did you ever choose this mountainside location in the first place? It's very small and wouldn't get a lot of sunshine in the winter."

Mihi answered, "We chose it because of its advantages. Here we have electricity, clean water and a septic system. And there are only two ways in. One of them is down the road that we came in on. The other is through the railway tunnel that goes under the ridge. The tunnel was built long ago for a small train to bring in men and materials for the construction of this dam as a water reservoir for the city. There used to be a third track down the side of the ridge to the left of the tunnel entrance but a massive landslide turned a large segment of that track into a sheer rock wall. And a fourth track, which came in to the other side of the dam, is now totally overgrown with gorse, sown there by the men soon after we moved here."

"But why live here at all? Wouldn't you be better out in the wide-open spaces, scattered all around the place?" Ricky went on.

"We considered that," said Mihi, "but we each need homes in close proximity to each other so we can operate a school, have our community meetings, and meet on Sabbaths for worship."

"This Sabbath thing is big with you, isn't it?" challenged Rick.

"It gives us regular periods for building and strengthening the values which form the foundation of our families and community. If you can think of anything better than the Sabbath for doing that, let me know," smiled Mihi confidently.

"Horse told me that the community spends several days each week out in the valley," Rick said. "Do you have a regular schedule that you all work to?"

"Yes," replied Mihi. "We all come back to the settlement at midday Friday, to get ready for the Sabbath. There are meals to prepare and houses to get ready. On Sabbath morning we meet for prayer from seven to eight, then we have breakfast. Our church service starts at ten-thirty in the morning and goes to noon. We have a break for three hours, during which people siesta, or play instruments together in the village band, or whatever. Afterwards, we have all-age Bible classes for ninety minutes, followed by a community meal.

"School for the children starts on Sunday, and runs for two and a half days. We also have our Council meeting, adult education programmes and a limited range of sports that day. On Monday, we do community work such as maintenance on the road, rail tracks and rolling stock, and community buildings. Tuesday morning is the time for attending to personal matters such as your home, or doing your own thing. At mid-afternoon on Tuesday, the train takes everyone, except the very old and sick and their care-givers and rostered security personnel, out of the valley to tend their gardens. That gives people about three days caring for fruit trees, gardens, or animals. Some of our people have other responsibilities out of the valley. I'll show you when you are well enough to travel."

"If you don't leave the valley until Tuesday, what were you doing over where we met on Sunday?" Rick asked.

"Each week a different family has the responsibility of providing meat for the village to cover the 'residency' days—that's from Friday afternoon til Tuesday night. We found it works best that way. Otherwise, a small family that killed a steer would have a problem disposing of all the meat, or keeping it fresh. My family supplied a large ostrich but it turned out to be insufficient so I got permission to go and hunt some wild pigs that had been seen down by the Lower Nihoputu dam."

"You went hunting wild pigs by yourself?" asked Rick incredulously.

"Yes. Why not? I do it all the time. It's not dangerous if you know what you are doing. I have to admit, though, that some people have no idea how to handle a wild pig," she smiled mischievously.

"You're not wrong," grinned Rick patting his sore rear.

"I wanted that boar because it was feral, and feral meat is good because it is low fat."

"I heard the Bible taught that pork is unclean," commented Rick.

"Yes, it's true that the Jews regarded pig meat as unclean, but Jesus said to His followers in Mark 7:14-23 that whatever you eat doesn't make you either acceptable or unacceptable to God because it passes right through your body into the loo. What makes people unclean are their thoughts and actions."

Rick and Mihi walked down the tracks for a few minutes until they came to a concrete structure built into the cliff face. "This is our power house and electrician's shop," said Mihi. "A pipeline from the dam now runs a turbine to produce power for the settlement. It is the pride of Kelly, our electrician. We needed electricity for heating and lighting, as well as cooking and refrigeration."

Rick's leg began to ache so he asked Mihi if she would mind if they called it a day. She apologised for being so inconsiderate, and saw him back to Horse's cabin with the promise to take him out of the valley the next day if he was up to it.

— o —

Early next morning, Horse had Rick at the line in time for the first train out to the flat lands. Mihi was there waiting for him. A small diesel engine pushing open carriages on which people sat back-to-back, facing outwards, came to them from the tunnel where it was stored. All who were waiting there climbed aboard and were taken through the tunnel out towards the area that Mihi called Swanson. At the station they stepped down from the train, which was then returned to the tunnel.

Near the place where the train left them was a large implement shed in which the vehicles belonging to the people were stored. Here Mihi had another quad bike, apparently her favourite vehicle.

"Let's go to the Quartermaster's Store first," she said.

"Sounds very army," Rick commented.

The Quartermaster's Store was nearby in what was once a large fruit packing shed. The husband-and-wife team, Quincy and Nancy, fussed over Rick as they showed him around. The walls were lined with deep shelves that contained cartons of gear and clothing, carpet squares and bolts of cloth. There was a heavy smell of mothballs in the air. One rack contained an assortment of rifle and shotguns, and cartons of ammunition. There were saddles and bridles, soccer balls and baseball gear. The centre of the store had a couple of never-used quad bikes, a six-seater ATV (All-Terrain Vehicle), several mountain bikes, buckets, brooms and various tools. Quincy told Rick that people in the village were not permitted to loot gear for themselves. If they wanted an item that wasn't in stock, they had to present their request in writing to the quartermaster, together with a deposit equal to a quarter of its value. Once this had been done, a special team picked up the item for them. It was then held in trust until they paid for it.

"Isn't that a bit restrictive?" Rick asked. "If the gear is out there for the taking, why not make use of it? And why pay for it?"

"That gear belongs to someone," said Nancy. "While that person may be dead, many will have relatives overseas who will, one day, want to claim their family's property. So we leave a record of what we have taken, and we keep another record here."

"Yeah, but why pay for it? By the time a new wave of immigrants comes to New Zealand all this stuff will be obsolete anyway."

"We are also thinking of our own people. Spider taught us that galleons of Aztec gold destroyed Spain. With their new-found wealth, few Spaniards bothered to work, train or study. It made the country lazy. As a result, Spain degenerated from being a leading nation in the Old World into a country with little influence on the international scene. We want our kids to grow up with a good work ethic and not believe the world owes them a living, for that would be a totally unrealistic view of life. Privilege must always be balanced by responsibility."

Rick was impressed. "What do you use for money?" he asked.

"We use the New Zealand metric currency; dollars and cents. And workers earn six dollars per hour. Anyone from the age of twelve can earn an income. Those who have made the effort to develop skills earn more in their area of expertise. This method encourages people to work and improve their talents. And if a person doesn't work, he doesn't eat."

"What about the old people? I saw a few of them."

"One way people in the community can get an income is by caring for the old folk and anyone having an injury or illness that prevents them from looking after themselves. They maintain and clean their houses, and provide food for them from the communal gardens. The old folk also get a pension from the community fund. Everyone here gives eight hours work a week to the community as their tax. Most people do their tax service on Mondays."

"Who are those two young men working here with you?" Rick asked.

"They are both on bail for wrongs committed," said Quincy. "I would have introduced you to them but they are not allowed to talk with anyone until their sentences are finished."

Next, Mihi took Rick to see the Builder's shed where he spent an hour plumbing the depths of Chippy's knowledge about boats. He was pleased to discover that he had done boat work for one other would-be escaper from New Zealand's shores. Rick mentioned to him that he would like to get over to one of the marinas on the Waitemata Harbour to check out the boats there.

"You can forget that idea!" retorted Chippy.

"What do you mean?" Rick asked.

"At the time of the big earthquake, this month three years ago, there was a huge tidal wave on the east coast. Must have peaked at about twelve metres. It flooded into the harbours, bays and estuaries, ripping all the boats from their moorings and marinas and smashing them into matchwood among the trees and houses. No doubt you would have experienced it in Australia, to a reduced degree."

"Yeah, I remember that. Wasn't anything like you had here, though. All we got was some very annoying erosion on our eastern coastline and beaches." Rick paused, deep in thought, then bounced back, "But not all boats would have been in the water. There must be some in backyards and other places where they had been taken for maintenance work."

"True. We have located a few good ones. And we have put covers over them to protect them from the weather. But there is the problem of getting them to the water. As soon as you start moving a big vehicle like a boat-hauler, it's going to be picked up by a spy-plane. The photos they take each day are probably compared with earlier photos to see what has changed. They will then track the boat and sink it out at sea. They have all the exits covered."

"Seems like it, doesn't it?"

After that Rick did a lot of thinking about these boats and how he might get one of them to the water without being detected.

Mihi then took him on to the mechanic's workshop, which was originally a service station, but Watson, the mechanic, wasn't in. They spent the rest of the day looking at farmland where there were horses, sheep, cattle, deer, goats, ostriches, alpacas, hens and turkeys. Even though the larger birds did a reasonable job of spreading the dry dung, many of the paddocks clearly needed harrowing and ploughing, for the grass looked quite rank. Manuka and gorse were growing back across the farmland. Mihi told Rick that they couldn't make any major changes to the land lest the contrast between the cultivated land and the rest of the country became obvious in spy-plane photographs. One advantage they had was that there was plenty of land and the animals were free to move themselves to the best grazing.

That evening, Rick stayed in a farmhouse with J.B. and his housemate, Gisborne Jones, who was affectionately known as Giz. The sunset sky was clear of cloud but it glowed an unearthly mauvey-bronze colour. The next morning a fine white ash, carried in by a southerly breeze settled over everything. It coated the leaves of the trees and shrubs, and lay like a dusting of fine snow on the paddocks, housetops, and roads. Giz thought it was from a large bush or scrub fire. J.B. reckoned there had been too much rain recently for that. It wasn't until that evening, when a reconnoitring party of four men returned from a trip to Raglan, that everyone learned the cause of these mysteries. The four men had witnessed large plumes of smoke rising from Mount Taranaki by day, and the glow of fire at its summit by night. Fortunately for everyone, the wind direction changed the next day and the ash didn't bother them again.

On Thursday evening, J.B. told Rick about the days immediately after the community had been established.

"There was general concern about the suffering of farm animals as water supplies began to fail," he explained, "It was decided that the best thing that could be done, in the circumstances, would be to tie back the gates and cut as many fences as possible to let the animals roam free. Every day teams went out on this mission. At first they used helicopters to get to distant farms. The deceased butcher, Costello, had a chopper licence, so they flew the choppers from Whenuapai and Ardmore until the helicopters ran out of hours and became potentially unsafe.

"An engineer (also deceased) then created some automatic fence-cutters that he mounted on the bull-bars of six four-wheel drive vehicles. Each fence cutter consisted of two face-to-face blades of steel mounted vertically in the centre of the bull-bar, with their leading edges facing forward, like your hands held together, palm to palm, with fingers pointing skywards. When the vehicle was driven at a fence at about ten kilometres per hour, the saw-teeth fed the fence wires into these miniature key-holes. The force of the collision with the fence wires forced both blades backwards against compression springs. Each blade travelled in its own guides: one travelled back, and upwards a centimetre; the other travelled back and down a centimetre, thus severing the wires. They were very efficient devices when kept well-greased. The front mud guards of the vehicles took a bit of a battering from flying fence battens but it was a small price to pay for the freedom of the animals. Each fence cutter vehicle worked together with four young people in a support vehicle. Their job was to collect canned, bottled and packet food from the empty houses, to organise accommodation, and provide drinks, meals, back-up staff, spare tyres and fuel.

"They operated in four-hour shifts from daylight til dark every day until just before Christmas. In those days the roads were in top condition, which enabled them to cover a lot of ground throughout Te Ika Amaui (the North Island). Today, there are large herds of cattle, deer and horses roaming over the pasturelands. The sheep however, hadn't fared very well, as packs of wild dogs ran amok, killing them for killing's sake. What sheep remained were now very wild and restricted to the high country where dogs rarely went."

Rick was asleep before J.B. had finished his summary.

The next day, J.B. took Rick in his Ute to an old orchard to pick several boxes of apples. They took them back to Waitak where they had electricity to cook and bottle them for winter. On Saturday, Rick, not being religious, excused himself from going to church and went for a walk instead, up to the dam and out into the bush on the other side. He didn't want to offend his hosts, but as they put no pressure on him to attend their services, he preferred to be by himself. He couldn't help noticing, though, the look of disappointment on Mihi's face. By the time he returned to the settlement, late that afternoon, he had hatched a plan for his getaway.

CHAPTER FOUR

On Sunday, Rick and Mihi got permission to leave the settlement to look at boats that were in people's yards. They went on Mihi's quad bike. At their first stop Rick asked rather crisply, "Why can't you folk be like normal people and go to church on Sunday?"

"What if it's not normal to go to church on Sunday?" responded Mihi.

"Outside New Zealand it's normal."

"It might be usual, but it's not normal."

"What do you mean by that?"

"Normal means 'in accordance with established norms or principles.' There's no law principle in the Bible stating that folk should remember Sunday to keep it holy. On the contrary, biblical Law says, 'Remember the seventh day to keep it holy.' And, according to the dictionary and standard calendars, the seventh day of the week is Saturday."

"Isn't that being a bit legalistic?"

"No more so than requiring voting church members to be baptised, or couples who wish to live together to get married."

"But wasn't the Sabbath changed to Sunday with the death of Jesus?"

"No."

"Look, I'm no theologian," admitted Rick, "but I always understood that Jews kept the seventh-day of the week, but Christians kept the first day."

"Well, according to Dad, who researched this matter quite extensively, that argument is based on a common misconception."

"And what might that be?"

"That the Jews and the early Christians were two different groups when they weren't. All the early Christians were Jews, and when three thousand were converted on the day of Pentecost they just didn't suddenly cease being Jews. They were regarded by everyone as just another Jewish sect. The only difference between these Christian Jews and all other Jews is that the Christians accepted Jesus as their Messiah. In everything else they remained essentially Jewish. Furthermore, these early Christians continued worshipping at the Temple and that involved Sabbath worship."

"What about the Gentile Christians? I understand that they couldn't worship at the temple."

"Not true! The temple had a special court for the Gentiles to worship in."

"But I was told that the Gentiles were Sunday-keepers."

"You were told wrong. The only Scriptures the early Christians had was the Old Testament. This Bible, which the apostle Paul said was 'useful for teaching and correcting' says, in Isaiah 56, that all non-Jews who came to the Lord and who kept the Sabbath without desecrating it, would be accepted by him. Besides, the New Testament clearly reveals that the Gentile and Jewish believers worshipped together, so that would exclude two different worship days."

"What about the argument that Sunday celebrates the resurrection of Jesus?"

"I thought the resurrection of Jesus was celebrated every Easter."

Rick thought about that for a few moments. "Yeah, that's a point," he said. "Who has birthday every week? Hey! It's time we moved off."

They inspected six boats, but none of them suited Rick's plan. They either had steel hulls or steel superstructure, or auxiliary engines. He wanted a boat that was entirely wooden, with a wooden mast and no engine.

They returned to the village and put in an order with Quincy for such a vessel. It was two weeks before one was found. They went out to Beach Haven to see it and Rick gauged that it was as near-perfect for his purpose as he could wish. He spent some time running a tape measure over it, with Mihi on the other end. Rick then drew up some rough sketches to outline his plans for this particular vessel.

As he stood there gazing at his outlines, deep in thought, Mihi gently took his hand in hers. He suddenly became aware of the fact that there was another influence taking priority in his life alongside his plans to return home to Australia. He turned and smiled at her, before slipping his hand free to nervously fold up his sketches.

On the way back to the settlement, conflicting emotions surged through Rick. Mihi had asked him to drive the quad, and she sat behind with her arms wrapped tightly around his waist and her cheek against his right shoulder. Here was this beautiful woman tugging at his heartstrings and giving him every reason to stay, yet there was an equally powerful urge within him to get back to Queensland.

While parked under some trees, during the time the spy in the sky flew overhead, Rick discussed his escape plans with Mihi. They agreed that it was essential to get the support of the whole community, through the Council, for his project. That night they drafted a letter asking permission for Rick to speak to the Council at its meeting the following Sunday morning.

The next morning Rick helped Mihi at the school. He made three new desks for her class and painted them. At Mihi's request, he gave a couple of lessons on Australian geography to the children in the upper grades. He thought he was doing quite well until a youth raised his hand and said, "Excuse me, Mr. Carter, why do you Australians hate us and want to kill us?"

Rick coughed and replied, "Australians don't hate you. They don't even know that you exist. It seems that there are some officials in the Australian government and armed forces who know that there are still people in New Zealand, but who are afraid that they are carriers of the Leoenzide virus. Knowing how the 1918-19 influenza pandemic killed many millions of people world-wide, they decided not to take any chances with this devastating plague."

"But we are not disease-carriers, sir!"

"You and I know that. But they don't. It is my opinion that the only thing that will save you is for someone to escape from this country to take the truth about you people to the rest of the world. You will continue to live under a shadow until that happens."

"Are you going to save us, sir? My father says you have plans to get away on a boat."

"Yes, that is my goal."

"Would you like us to pray for you, sir?"

"Well, uh, yeah, that would be good of you."

At the end of that class period, Spider asked him if he would mind teaching the same students the following week, on the history of human settlement in Australia. Rick, however, felt that it was more important that he take some classes on basic grammar, as the years of isolation had resulted in some divergences in pronunciation and spelling. These needed to be corrected so that the New Zealanders did not fall behind the changes that had taken place in the rest of the English-speaking world. There were also new words in use that Kiwis didn't yet know about. Spider not only agreed with him but said he would like to attend these classes himself.

On Wednesday, as Carla was removing Rick's stitches, he asked her about the incidence of disease and accident in the community. She replied, "There are hardly any degenerative disease such as diabetes, heart disease, cancer or prostate problems, here. The natural diet and active lifestyles free of constant stress are the main factors in precluding the physical and emotional problems that afflict the Western consumer society. We've had three broken limbs and a broken collarbone as a result of falls from horses, a scalding, some axe wounds, several infections, plus a man who got a punctured lung when his quad bike rolled on him two years ago. He has been our only fatality. We thought we had saved him, but he got a bad infection and died."

"I'm sad to hear that. Did he have a wife and children?"

"No, fortunately. He was engaged to be married to Mihi. It's taken her this long to get over it. Seems like she has found someone else, though."

Rick blushed but said nothing.

Rick didn't have to do much talking at the Council meeting. They said they would give him whatever help he needed but warned him of the dangers of trying to break through the cordon around the country. They told him what he had already heard from others, that every day a turbo-prop aircraft went up and down the coasts on both sides, and submarines patrolled both the Tasman Sea and the Pacific Ocean. They had also seen lines of buoys anchored off some harbours. No one was quite sure what these buoys detected, but they probably had a purpose in keeping New Zealand isolated.

Rick thanked them for their concern, and told them how much he appreciated their kindness to him. It was a debt that he could only repay by escaping to reveal the truth about their circumstances. What he needed was the loan of their community carpenter, plus an assistant for about two months. He would also need tools and materials.

"You can have Chippy as soon as he has finished the new roof on the Watson's home," said Cardiac Porter. "At the rate he's going, it shouldn't take him more than two or three days to complete that job."

Indicating the quartermaster with a nod of his head, Cardiac continued, "Give your list of materials and tools required to Quincy here. The Council has agreed to finance your project from its own funds."

That night, after the evening meal, Rick went to see to see Chippy, taking his sketches with him. He laid them out on the table and told him that he wanted to cut down the superstructure of the boat so that it was no more than forty centimetres above the waterline. The cabin inside was deep enough to permit this. "What you want is not a boat but a submarine," remarked Chippy. "Just how do you propose to get in and out of this boat in rough seas without sinking it?"

"Yeah, that's a good question, but I believe we can do it. I have this idea. We'll build two hatches to the area below the upper deck: a larger hatch up front for provisioning and servicing the boat in harbour, and a small hatch with a sliding lid near the stern, just big enough for a person to get through in their wet-weather gear. Beneath the small hatch we'll build a watertight pod, large enough to accommodate one person. If this fills up with water when I'm going on deck, it won't matter much. It can just stay filled until I go below again. Once that hatch has been closed and fastened, a valve will be opened to release the water into the bilge from where it can be pumped overboard."

"How do you propose to steer the boat?"

"Well, down below there will be a conventional wheel, but on top I will install some ropes and pulleys, connected to the tiller. These ropes will be flush with the outer-edges of the stern deck. It is my plan to keep down below and thus be out of sight most of the time. For this reason, I want to keep the sail very simple so it can be controlled from below decks. I also want to keep the boat's above-water profile as low as possible to avoid detection by radar. We will paint it in matt camouflage colours and there will be no metal fittings bar the absolute essentials. I want it to be all but invisible from over four-hundred metres on a grey day."

"That's a tall order, but I believe we can do it."

"Good on yer, mate. You'd make a dinkum Aussie," said Rick, slapping Chippie on the back.

"I'm not so sure that I'd want to be an Aussie, pal."

"Let me assure you, Chippy, the ones you're thinking about right now aren't dinkum Aussies."

Rick arranged with the quartermaster for the supplies to be delivered to an address in Beach Haven where a suitable yacht had been found. It was under a corrugated lean-to against a house.

Once the lean-to had been made weatherproof, they tackled the major task of cutting the boat down to its planned size. The superstructure was removed with the help of a skill saw powered by a portable generator. They dismantled the structure carefully and stored what they didn't need under the house. To make their work easier they then decided to cut a large doorway in the wall of the house. This proved to be an excellent idea as it gave them good access to the boat and meant that their tools could be stored inside.

The house was set up as a temporary camp, and the two men plus Westie, their helper, agreed to stay there from Monday evening till midday Friday each week. Before the men moved in, Mihi set about getting rid of thirty years of dusty cobwebs and grime to make the house habitable.

Over the next two weeks they worked long hours refitting the interior of the yacht. A strong plastic water tank was boxed in firmly enough to withstand the boat rolling over, and the cabin was fitted with small cupboards that wouldn't spring open in big seas. A twelve-volt battery and wiring for lighting were installed, and Kelly gave Rick a wind-powered generator that could be mounted in a bracket on the upper deck. This generator would keep the battery charged and supply light inside. A set of laminated charts of the South Pacific was provided by the Quartermaster's Store, plus two hand-powered water pumps.

The remaking of the superstructure proved to be the most difficult operation of all. Finding and transporting the right timbers to the site was slow, but little by little the top sides began to take shape. Chippy was thorough if not fast. He insisted that every joint be absolutely perfect. The days were getting noticeably shorter with the approach of mid-winter so less could be done. On certain overcast days the lighting in the shelter was poor due to a nearby stand of fir trees. Rick wanted to cut the trees down but Chippy said that would be very unwise and could jeopardise their project. The disappearance of the trees could be picked up by computerised systems that were able to differentiate between photographs taken by spy planes on successive days.

On Tuesday, one week before they decided to call it quits for the rest of winter, Mihi turned up at midday on her trail bike. She had the day off from teaching school and said she wanted to see how the boat was progressing. Rick was glad to see her, and showed her over the vessel. She had brought some fresh vegetables and venison with her and set about making a stew for their tea. While they were still eating, she asked Rick, "Do you still want to leave?"

"I have to, Mihi, for your sake as well as everyone else's."

A tear formed in the corner of her eye, which she brushed away with the ball of her thumb. Mihi didn't say any more until they were washing up. While doing the dishes she told Rick that her dad had recommended that the Council bring Draper back from the Coromandel. He said that Draper had been in exile for ten years, and that he felt the time had now come to show the man some humanity by offering him the support and fellowship of the community. Surprisingly, there were no objections.

"The plan is to take six people in three ATV's towing trailers, plus two security personnel, J.B. and Gisborne Jones, who would accompany the group on their trail bikes. We will go to Thames to harvest the ripe macadamia nuts at a plantation there. We expect to return with at least a trailer load of dried nuts. The Council chairman also wants us to bring back some gold from the office of the gold mine there."

"What on earth would you do with gold?" asked Rick. "You can't eat it."

"You'll have to ask him about that," Mihi laughed. "Anyway, I've got permission for you to come. That's if you want to?"

"I'd love to. When does the expedition depart?"

"Next Wednesday morning."

"That's a convenient coincidence," said Rick. Chippy and I have decided, because of the constant rain over the last few weeks, to leave further work on the boat until mid-August. Furthermore, if spy plane surveillance has picked up any activity around here, a break of a few weeks may turn their attention away from this site. I also know that Chippy would like a break to be with Caroline and their new baby."

That Friday evening Mihi had asked Rick if he would attend church with her the next day. He told her that he respected her religious values, but the idea of going to church on Saturday seemed a bit sectarian to him. His refusal disappointed her again, but she left the matter there and didn't pursue it any further.

CHAPTER FIVE

Early on Wednesday morning, Horse shook Rick awake to a steaming breakfast set on the table for him. The forthcoming trip with the team to the Coromandel Peninsula had Rick bubbling with excitement.

The journey to Thames took two days. With a small manual pump that they carried with them, they extracted fuel from underground tanks at service stations along the road. While the fuel was old, it still worked remarkably well. The first day of their journey they used their chainsaw twice to cut their way through trees that had fallen across the road.

At the meal that evening in a house beside the road, Rick found himself sitting next to Spider.

"What's your religious background, Rick?" asked Spider.

"Got none," offered Rick. "Only went to church once. For a wedding. I learned what little I know through arguing with Christians at university, and by osmosis from the Bible-in-Schools teacher who used to take the Bible lesson in my class every Wednesday morning at the primary school where I teach."

"Used to?"

"Yeah, Bible in schools was eventually squeezed out of the curriculum as there was no time for it."

"Any Christians in your extended family?"

"Yes. My grandmother was a Christian, through and through. I respected her, even though she was a bit unusual."

"In what way?"

"She kept telling me about a dream she had of me. I think it was about my death."

"Your death?"

"Yes. In her dream she saw me being lowered into a cloud and the angels were singing."

"That was it?"

"That was it. In every other way she was a good woman that people looked up to. Though, like most Christians, she went to church on Sunday."

"You've got a bit of a problem with the Saturday Sabbath, haven't you?" mentioned Spider in a quiet, non-threatening tone.

"You could say that. If Saturday Sabbath is so right, why do most Christians go to church on Sunday?"

"Most people used to believe that the earth was flat."

"Okay . . . so you're saying numbers don't make it right."

"You've got it."

"Well, if these Sunday-keepers are so wrong, why does God bless them as much as he does?"

"God indeed blesses his people who go to church on Sunday, just as he blessed and cared for the Hebrews during their forty years in the wilderness. But he now wants them to move on to even greater blessings."

Rick, with his elbows on the table and his hot drink clasped in both hands, went silent. Spider could see that he was in deep thought. After a while Rick put his mug down and asked, "If all the early

Christians kept the seventh-day Sabbath, how come most folk go to church on Sunday and not on Saturday today? Why did they change from keeping the Sabbath to going to church on Sunday?"

"Rick, that same question also troubled me. I spent many, many hours in two Auckland theological libraries searching through books and other data on early church history for the answer. And this is what I discovered: Saturday was the only day observed widely as the weekly worship day for up to four generations after Jesus. There is no evidence that Sunday was kept as a regular worship day before AD 135."

"What happened in AD 135?"

"The change to Sunday worship came about as a reaction to fundamentalist Jews. The radical Jews of that time were like the Jihadi Muslims of more recent times. They believed that they and they alone were God's people, and their hand was against every non-Jew, especially their Roman overlords. In many places they started riots and insurrections that resulted in tens of thousands of deaths. Emperor Hadrian would have had peace throughout the entire Roman Empire if it weren't for these radical Jews who were fighting for their independence from Rome. In response Hadrian imposed additional taxes on the Jews to cover the costs of the extra legions needed to keep them under control. He also forbade the observance of the seventh-day Sabbath.

"As you can imagine, that became a real problem for Christians also, because they weren't looked upon as being separate from the Jews, as they are today. Just as there were the Pharisee Jews, and the Sadducee Jews, and Essene Jews back then, so there were also Christian Jews. Their leader was a Jew, the apostles were all Jews, the Christian Scriptures were Jewish, and the Christian worship days were Jewish. So when the government cracked down on the rebellious Jews and penalised them with extra taxes and forbade Sabbath observance, the Christians copped it in the neck too.

"In Rome and Alexandria—two main centres in the Old World—the Christians decided the time had come to sever their relationship with Judaism. The churches in these two cities, in their haste to get as far away as possible from anything Jewish, began to worship on the popular Roman holiday, *Dies Solis*, or the day of the sun. The Alexandrian Christians were already meeting at sunrise on Sundays, in honour of Jesus' resurrection, so it was no big thing to extend their worship time on the first day of the week by a few hours. From the time of Jesus, Saturn had been worshipped as the chief Roman god, so Saturday was the Roman rest day. But when Saturn was displaced by *Dies Solis*, Saturn's day (Saturday) was replaced by Sunday as the Roman rest day. Furthermore, it was now more convenient for the Roman Gentiles to attend church on their day off, which was then Sunday."

"That was the start of Sunday worship?"

"Pretty much. In time other churches began worshipping on Sundays too, but, unlike the churches in Rome and Alexandria, which gave up the Sabbath, Christians elsewhere continued to keep the seventh day of the week as the Sabbath."

"Are you telling me that outside of Rome and Alexandria, Christians went to church two days a week—on Saturdays as well as Sundays?"

"Yep! The churches outside Rome catered for the Christian Jews on Saturdays, and for Christian Gentiles on Sundays. And they did so for hundreds of years."

"How is it, then, that the Sabbath eventually disappeared and Sunday won out as the universal worship day?"

"As you will know from your own reading of history, the church in Rome grew in power and eventually dominated the other churches in the old world. Wherever missionaries from Rome went, they made it their policy to evangelise the rulers before they evangelised the people. It was these 'converted' rulers who enforced the Roman Sunday as the Christian day of worship, and who persecuted other Christians that worshipped on the seventh-day Sabbath. That is what happened throughout mainland Europe, England, Wales, Scotland and Ireland."

"I didn't know that."

"There's one thing you should know, young man, and that is nobody will be saved just because they observe the seventh-day Sabbath. Judas, along with Jesus' other disciples, was a Sabbath-keeper, but he won't be in the heavenly kingdom because, unlike the others, he didn't accept Jesus as his Lord and Saviour. You will be saved only if you put your faith in Jesus who died for you. Once you have done that, your resting on the Sabbath will signify that you are resting in Jesus' finished work for you on the cross."

Yawning, he continued. "Well, I'm not as young as you and I need my sleep, so I'm off to get some shut-eye. See you in the morning."

The next day, while crossing the Piako River bridge, they disturbed a herd of nine elephants that were bathing in the water and rolling in the mud. The matriarch of the herd raised her trunk in their direction and tasted the air. When the human intruders did not retreat, she came forward a few paces and trumpeted loudly. Rick turned to Mihi with a question mark on his face. Mihi explained that at the height of the plague the Auckland Zoo authorities had the dangerous and helpless animals in their care put down, but released the elephants. These pachyderms had made this area their calving grounds for the past few years.

Later that day, as they approached Thames, they could see that the lower part of the town had filled with rocks, stones, sand and tree trunks that had been carried there by the Kauaeranga River in flood.

Spider suggested that the party split into two equal groups: one should leave to gather macadamia nuts at the plantation down the road, while the other would start a search for Draper. However, when evidence of Draper's presence was picked up early next morning, in the form of motorcycle tyre prints in dried mud—prints that had not been washed away by recent rain—everyone agreed that both parties should search for Draper, and having found him, then go together for the nuts. The group divided into two to look around the town for any other signs that could lead them to Draper.

It was mid-afternoon when they all got together again down by the waterfront. No one had any promising signs to report so they agreed to check out the area bordering the coast road that went north along the eastern side of the Firth of Thames. They assumed that Draper wouldn't have moved too far away from the sea or the main road.

At some distance from the town Rick, Mihi and J.B. chose a side road that followed a stream coursing down from the eastern hills towards the Firth. After a fruitless search of the houses up the road they returned to a point not far from the coast where their road rose up over a bluff on the southern side of the stream. They had just switched off their engines to discuss their next move when they heard the sound of an outboard motor. Through their binoculars they could clearly see a Zodiac RIB (Rubber Inflatable Boat), with three men in blue-grey overalls on board, coming up the Firth, in their direction.

"Who do you think they are?" asked Mihi, as she passed her binoculars to Rick.

"I have no idea," replied J.B. "They don't appear to be expecting any trouble though, otherwise they'd be holding weapons. I just hope that Giz and his party stays out of sight. It could be very awkward if his group turned up now."

The Zodiac swung in towards the mouth of the stream.

"If they aren't from the Auckland settlement, and if you don't recognise them as someone from Keri Keri, then there is a strong possibility that they are Australian military personnel, wouldn't you say?" Rick asked.

There was no reply.

The RIB beached and the men got out and towed it upstream, under the bridge of the coastal road, to a point on the other side of the stream just a hundred metres or so from the bluff they were on. After tugging their boat up onto a shingle bank one of them went into the bush to relieve himself while another got out a notebook or map. He was in the process of pointing out something up the valley to his companion when both men froze. At that same instant the man who had gone into the bush came running out doing up his belt. They had heard Giz and his party coming back down the coastal road on their return journey to Thames. Giz had a trail bike with a very noisy exhaust-pipe, and in the quiet early winter afternoon its reverberations echoed around the hills.

The three men conferred, one of them ran to their craft, picked up a gun a and raced to hide up in the trees on the bank. The other two just crouched by their rubber boat in the late afternoon shade and waited. The three ATVs roared across the bridge over the stream and continued south on the coastal road. There was no sign that they had seen the Zodiac and the two men crouching by it.

After the Giz and his party had gone the third man came out of the bush and there was a very agitated conversation among all three. Rick turned to say something to J.B. and noticed that Mihi wasn't there.

"Where's Mihi?" he whispered, almost in a panic.

J.B. shrugged his shoulders but didn't look concerned.

"I'm going to find her," Rick said with a determined look.

J.B. put a restraining hand on Rick's arm. "Mihi is able to look after herself. I'd advise you to stay put. She won't be too pleased if you blow her cover. Look!" he said, pointing back up the valley road.

Rick could see Mihi at a point where the road and stream curved around behind them. Out of sight of the three men that had come ashore in the Zodiac, she waded across the stream into the bush on the other side. Rick guessed that she would come back, under the cover of the bush, to a point close to where the three men were.

"I'd give my eye teeth to find out who those chaps are, where they have come from and why they are here," Rick muttered.

"If you are patient, Mihi might be able to tell you," advised J.B. quietly.

The visitors were now engaged in a heated discussion, and every now and then Rick and J.B. were able to pick up a word or two. Several minutes later they stopped talking and walked back down the side of the stream towards the bridge. They hadn't gone far when Rick and J.B. saw Mihi slip out of the bush with a sheath knife in her hand. She stabbed Zodiac in several places; grabbed a semi-automatic rifle and a box of ammunition from inside and, just as silently, slipped back into the shadows. At the bridge the men climbed cautiously up onto the road and looked along it both ways. Suddenly one of them swore at the top of his voice and pointed back to their deflated vessel on the sand. The three jumped into the streambed and raced back. The one with the gun pointed to a footprint in a wet patch of sand among the pebbles. Looking up at the bush he raised his gun to his hip and fired off a burst of bullets.

"Good!" whispered J.B.

"What do you mean, 'good!'?" asked Rick rather crossly. "Mihi is in there!"

"Uh, uh. She'll be well away. The more shots he fires off, the less ammo he has left."

When Mihi emerged from the bush upstream around the bend, Rick ran to meet her. "I was terrified that they might have shot you," he blurted out. He took her hand to help her back up the bank to the road. While she didn't need the help, she gladly accepted it.

"Let's get back to J.B." she said. "I've got something important you both need to hear."

Back on the bluff, Mihi told J.B. and Rick that she overheard the men arguing about the best way to find Draper's co-ordinates and get back to their submarine without being detected by the group in the ATVs.

"'Draper's co-ordinates can only mean one thing," she continued. "They have found Draper and he has the GPS locators for our Waitak settlement hidden somewhere. They have obviously come here to get it. That's why I had to prevent them from getting away until we were absolutely sure they didn't have those details. I'd dearly love to know how Draper discovered the location for our new settlement."

"Well," said J.B., "these three men have got a new dynamic to handle. They are now aware of the fact that someone knows they are here; their RIB is a no-go. They're also limited to one gun, and they won't be able to leave until tomorrow morning at the earliest. It's getting too late in the day for another boat to come and pick them up—if their submarine has another one, which I seriously doubt. We've already searched the houses up this road, without success, so I suggest that we let these men lead us to Draper's note listing the co-ordinates, then figure out how we can relieve them of it."

Back on the stream-bed the three men tugged their deflated boat and outboard behind a log that had been stranded on the shingle bank. They then covered it with branches and reeds.

"I have an idea," said Rick. "Because I'm an Aussie, with a very good reason for being here in New Zealand, I'm neutral. It's worth the risk to go and talk with them, don't you think?"

When the others hesitated, he added, "Keep me covered, just in case."

Rick ran back down the blindside of the bluff and, at the bottom, jumped into the stream, waded across and turned back toward the three men.

"Hey! Hey! Help!" he cried out.

The reaction was immediate. They dropped to their knees and the one with the gun aimed it at Rick. If Rick was afraid, he didn't show it. Stumbling towards them and waving both hands in the air to show that he wasn't armed, he called out, "Are you fellows Australians by any chance?"

"You sound like a dinkum Aussie to me, mate," said one of the three, getting to his feet as he addressed Rick. "How in the heck did you get here?"

"I'm Rick Carter from Port Douglas. My yacht got blown here by Cyclone Funi."

"We all thought you was drowned, mate. The search planes covered a huge area looking for you before they gave up. By the way, my name is Mace, this is Jordan and he's Spooner."

"Am I pleased to meet you!" said Rick, stepping forward and extending his hand. But all three stepped back, holding their hands up with their palms facing towards Rick.

"If you don't mind, we'd rather not have any contact," said one.

Rick noticed their names embossed in white on their overalls. Spooner, the one with the gun, asked, "Were you the one who knifed our Zodiac?"

"Don't be stupid," retorted Jordan. "That was a woman's footprint. Besides, he's wearing boots."

"Yeah," responded Spooner. "But he may know who the bitch is."

"Do you?" asked Jordan.

"Do I what?" stalled Rick.

"Do you know who slashed our inflatable?"

"You have an inflatable that someone has deflated?"

"Not deflated! Destroyed!" he almost shouted.

"It could have been one of the Maori who are living in this area," said Rick in a half lie. "They are pretty upset with the way they have been treated, and are out for revenge. 'Utu' they call it. I have to say, though, that they have been pretty good to me. I wouldn't have survived without their help."

"Where, exactly, do these Maori live?" asked Mace.

"They're nomads," replied Rick, thinking quickly. "They live off the land and sea."

"What about those motorbikes we saw?" asked Jordan.

"Aren't they a part of your group?" asked Rick in mock surprise.

"Nope."

"Well, where did you guys come from, then?" Rick asked in an attempt to change the subject.

His question was ignored.

"Do you know anybody by the name of Draper? asked Mace.

"Yes," replied Rick. "He's an old identity in these parts."

"Funny. He never said anything about other folk in this area. Reckoned he lived here all by himself."

"Yeah, that's Draper," laughed Rick. "He's a bit of a recluse. He would have been quite happy if we had all moved out and left him to himself. The way he handled it was to pretend that we didn't exist."

"Can you take us to his house?"

Rick cleared his throat. "Ah, which one? He laid claim to several homes. Which one he lives in depends upon the season and the fishing."

"He wanted us to pick up some things for him."

"Did he give you any description of the particular home?"

"Nope, but here are the directions to it," said Mace as he opened a flap on his overalls and extracted a small sheet of folded paper. When he unfolded the yellowing sheet, Rick saw immediately that it was a sketch of the road adjacent to the stream. There were three houses marked on the map and the nearest one was identified with a cross. He remembered that that particular house had been painted green and white and that it had a conservatory on the front. He also recalled that there was nothing in it to indicate that anyone had been living there.

"That house there," said Rick, turning and pointing with his finger, "is the one where Draper spends most of the winter. He likes it because it has a conservatory on the front to keep it warm at this time of the year. He's only just shifted in, though, so I don't expect that you will find much there."

"Come with us to it."

"The house is empty."

"We'd still like to see it."

"Okay," Rick shrugged, "but, as I told you, there's nothing there."

He led them up the stream until they had passed the bluff. He then re-crossed the stream to the road. Glancing back unobtrusively he could see that J.B. and Mihi had wheeled the bikes back over the crest of the road away from them and out of sight.

At the house Mace asked them to remain outside while he went indoors. In less than a minute he returned, patting a chest pocket. "I'm mighty obliged to you, Mr Carter," he said. "I have one more favour to ask of you. We have a good outboard motor, but no dinghy to get us back to our vessel. If you can get us a dinghy, we'll give you the outboard as a gift when we're finished with it."

"The only gift I want," said Rick, "is a ride back to Australia on your vessel."

"I'm sorry, we can't do that."

"Why not? If you can take Draper, you can take me. What's the difference?"

"Who said we are taking Draper?" sneered Spooner, who realised, immediately, that he had said the wrong thing when he noticed Mace's look of disapproval.

"I don't give the orders in matters such as these, Mr Carter. I just obey them," said Mace. "The best I can do is advise my superiors of your presence here. Now, I'd be obliged if you would show us where we could get a dinghy."

Rick remembered seeing an aluminium dingy underneath a house on the slope beside the coastal road not far from the stream mouth. But he couldn't let these men get away that quickly so he told them about the boat club building this side of Thames where there were several good aluminium dinghies. Mace didn't like the idea of going there because that was where the party on the ATVs seemed to be going. But they needed a dinghy so, as the sun was setting, they all set off towards Thames.

Rick consoled himself with the thought that once they had selected a dinghy, they would still need to get it back to their outboard. In the meantime, he hoped that J.B. would come up with a plan to retrieve Draper's coordinates from Mace.

They set off along the road south, surreptitiously leaving J.B. and Mihi behind on the bluff.

As soon as they were out of range of their voices. J.B. asked. "Did you hear that? They are going all the way back to Thames to get a suitable dinghy. We need to get there before them."

"About a kilometre inland up this road, beside the stream, there is a puriri tree on the right-hand side with several mailboxes beside it. A steel gate opens onto a private gravelled road that is a back route to Thames," offered Mihi, pointing to the east. "On our bikes we could easily beat them."

"Perfect," acknowledged J.B. "We'll give them a few minutes to get out of hearing range and then we'll move off."

Nobody spoke until Rick and his three countrymen came to a small settlement spread out around the coastal road. It was getting dark and Mace wanted to know why Rick was intent on taking them all the way into Thames when there was, in all likelihood, a good dinghy somewhere on one of the properties along the road.

"Yeah, there are dinghies here," Rick agreed, "But none that I would trust my life to. Most have perished after years of sun and rain. Your best bet would be to go on to the old Thames Boating Club that isn't too much further along the road. There you will have a choice of a number of aluminium boats that are still seaworthy, and not full of green water like these. There should also be a light aluminium trailer there on which you could bring the dinghy back to your outboard motor."

"Okay, let's keep moving," agreed Mace.

There wasn't much talk along the road, apart from Mace's questions about how Rick had kept himself alive since landing in New Zealand. Once, Mace stopped suddenly and held up his hand, bringing everyone behind him to a halt. He stood there listening with his head cocked on one side.

"What is it?" asked Rick.

"Thought I heard a motor," said Mace.

After a few moments he snorted and they started off again. Later, on the outskirts of Thames, Mace called a halt near a creek that tumbled down a rocky face at the side of the road. Thirsty from their long march they each cupped their hands and drank deeply of the cooling water.

"How come you never got Leoenzide?" Mace asked Rick, looking up from where he was squatting on his heels.

"The Maori taught me to keep away from the dogs and what to do if they came near," Rick replied. "They are the carriers. They're vicious animals that will attack anyone who approaches them. Just don't look them in the eye though or they'll fly at you. One bite and your number's up."

The three Australian men looked decidedly uncomfortable.

"It's getting too dark to do much more," said Mace, "so we'll find a secure place for the night, and pick up that dinghy and a trailer at first light."

At what used to be a car sale yard on the seaward side of the road, they chose an upstairs office that had both an external and internal stairway. It was sparse, but secure. Both Rick and the others were hungry, not having eaten since midday, but no one mentioned the fact. They just spread out, curled up on the floor, and tried to make themselves comfortable. Mace divided what was left of the night into three hour shifts and said he would keep watch for the first three hours. When his shift was up, he woke Jordan, who said he needed to go and relieve himself before he could take over. His big drink of water was creating urgency. Jordan opened the door, stood in the opening for a moment to focus his eyes, and then stumbled down the stairs into the car yard. Mace rubbed at a grimy window with the cuff of his shirt but it was a moonless, overcast night so he couldn't see much.

After what seemed like several minutes, Mace went to the door and called in a hiss, "Jordan! Get yourself up here. Now is not the time to be checking out antique cars."

But there was no response from Jordan.

"Jordan," he hissed again. "Where the hell are you?"

Coming back inside Mace lightly toed Spooner in the side, waking him.

"Spooner, get up! Jordan went outside for a piss and he's gone off somewhere. Go and find him. I'll cover you from the top of the stairs."

Rick, who had been unable to get to sleep for wondering when Giz and the others were going to do something, was now fully alert. When he saw that Mace was out on the landing he crawled on his hands and knees to the door that led to the internal stairway. He stood up and was about to open the door when Mace looked back inside and yelled, "Where the hell do you think you're going!?"

Just then there was a crash and a grunt from the car yard below. Mace leapt back out the door onto the landing swinging his gun left and right, peering into the gloom. It was just the opportunity that Rick needed. He opened the door, stepped through and slammed it shut after him then raced down the internal stairway. The door at the bottom was locked, but when he banged on it and called out, someone unbolted it and dragged him through before shutting and re-bolting it. Rick stumbled into the repair shop, nearly falling over Spooner who was lying face down on the floor with Giz holding a gun against his neck while his hands were being fastened behind his back with black plastic ties. To Rick's utter amazement, J.B. was there too. J.B, with his eyes on Rick, held an upraised finger against his pursed lips.

Mace, sensing that the enemy was staked out underneath, fired two shots through the floor. Giz leapt forward when a bullet went through the heel of his boot. He sat down quickly on the floor and ripped his boot off to examine his heel which had been grazed and was bleeding. They all kept deathly quiet.

After a few moments of intense silence, during which no one moved, J.B. signalled them to get Spooner onto his feet and to follow him. J.B. stuck his gun in Spooner's ribs and indicated that they would shoot him if he so much as uttered a whimper. With Rick following, they moved out of the building on Mace's blind side and crossed the road to a brick lawyer's office on the other side. J.B. then returned to his post at the car sale yard.

Inside the brick building, on the floor, was Jordan, also tied and gagged, watched over by Mihi. As soon as she saw Rick, her face lit up and she rushed over and gave him a hug.

Giz tied Spooner's ankles together, telling him, as he did so, that if he didn't co-operate both he and Jordan would be introduced to the local dog pack in their birthday suits. Then with the business end of his rifle tucked under Spooner's right ear, Giz proceeded to interrogate him.

 In response Spooner told him that they were from the submarine ANV (Australian Naval Vessel) Hammerhead. The previous day they had picked up a fellow by the name of Draper. Some time back Draper had sailed over to the Whangaparaoa Peninsula because he had discovered, from a map that he had found in the old Thames Citizens' Advice Bureau, that there had been an army camp on the end of the Peninsula across the estuary. Over at the army camp, with the help of a small generator, he got a radio transmitter going with which he was able to advise the Australian Military of his whereabouts. Two days later, on his way back in his sailing dinghy, the Australians intercepted him.

When Giz asked Spooner where Draper was now, Spooner said he 'accidentally' fell overboard and was drowned. They made no effort to save him, fearing that he may have been a carrier of the Leoenzide virus. But before his 'accident' he told them that he had revisited Auckland and followed a quad-bike back to the Settlement. After writing down its GPS co-ordinates he returned to the Coromandel.

"Right," said Giz to Rick as he tied a gag on Spooner. "This is what we will do. The other soldier with the gun—what's his name?"

"Mace."

"Mace. Okay. We'll give Mace a sample of our firepower, then invite him to surrender. We must, however, under no circumstances give him any idea that we are after that map. Rick, you stay here with Mihi and keep an eye on Jordan and Spooner."

Giz slipped out the door and conferred with J.B. The two men then took up positions at opposite diagonals of the car yard. Keeping out of sight, Giz cupped his hands around his mouth and called into the still night air, "Mace! Do you hear me Mace? You are surrounded. Any attempt to escape and we will shoot you. We are holding your fellow marines captive, and we have your other weapon and won't hesitate to use it if you try to either deceive or evade us. To show you we are not fooling, we are now going to fire a couple of harmless bursts into the air. Do not shoot back or we will take you out! Did you hear me?"

There was no reply from Mace.

Giz fired the first burst into the sky, and then from the other side of the building J.B. did the same.

"Mace. Leave your weapon on the floor and come down the outside stairs with your hands on your head. If you do as you are told we give you our word that we will help you return to your submarine at daylight."

On the other side of the road in the brick lawyer's office, Mihi and Rick were standing, facing each other, holding hands.

"I love you, Ricky. With all my heart I love you," said Mihi looking at Rick's lips and lifting her face to his.

"I love you, too, Mihi. You're the best thing that's ever happened to me." And he kissed her tenderly. It was the sweetest, most electrifying thing he had ever experienced. Waves of ecstasy raced up and down his body. Mihi clung tightly to him.

But, unnoticed by Rick and Mihi, Spooner and Jordan had wriggled back-to-back. Silently and quickly Spooner used a small knife that he had taken from a side pocket on his right trouser leg to cut the tie that bound Jordan's hands. Jordan then removed his gag and got himself to his feet that were still tied together. With two mighty kangaroo hops he reached the window, shattering it with a head butt. "Mace!" he bellowed into the night air, "they're after the co-ordinates!"

Rick wrenched himself away from Mihi and raced across the room to Jordan, but Spooner swung his legs around in front of him and brought him down hard. Mihi, leaping to Rick's aid, kicked Spooner firmly in the solar plexus, temporarily paralysing his diaphragm, making him curl up as he struggled to get a breath.

Then, very deliberately, she walked up to Jordan with a raised chair and felled him. Rick got up and raced to the door to try and find out what had happened outside. There was total silence, so he returned and helped Mihi to retie Jordan's hands.

In less than a minute Giz returned. "What happened in here?" he asked in a serious tone. "Did you two get distracted?"

Rick ignored his pointed question. "Were you able to get the co-ordinates?" he asked.

Giz held up a folded piece of paper with a smile. He then took out a box of matches and struck one. There was a flare of light and the paper burned to ash.

Putting his head out the door Giz called, "J.B., bring Mace over here. The three men can spend the rest of the night here by themselves. We've got their weapons; they could become the next meal for a pack of ravenous mongrels." He winked at Rick, then addressed the three sub-mariners. "We'll cut you free for the night, and if you are still here at daybreak, we'll bring you some breakfast. After you have eaten, we will take you and a good dinghy back to your outboard and get you on your way home. If, however, you are not here, we will know that you have made other plans. You are free to choose, but you are not free to choose the consequences. So think carefully before you act."

The next morning, just as it was getting light, Giz knocked on the office door. Jordan opened it. "We have some hot food for you," said Giz, motioning to Mihi to bring it in. She opened a container on one of the trailers and took out three plastic bowls with lids and carried them and three spoons to the door. "It's not what your chef would offer you for breakfast, but it's nutritious and tasty," she said as she passed the bowls over.

She went back out and returned with a large plastic bottle of water and three plastic cups.

"As soon as you are finished, we'll get moving," said Giz, who then shut the door behind him, leaving them to eat alone.

Ten minutes later the three men emerged, wiping their mouths. Three ATVs were waiting for them. A fourth one was towing a trailer with an inverted aluminium dinghy strapped to it.

"Thanks for the food," said Mace, licking his lips. "Never thought I'd enjoy a feed of veggies as much as that. Especially for breakfast. We appreciate your kindness."

J.B. invited each of them into an ATV.

The caravan moved off, with J.B. leading and Giz following in the rear.

At the bridge they put the dinghy into the water and towed it upstream to collect the outboard. As Jordan fastened the outboard motor to the dinghy, J.B. said, "You won't be able to get this dinghy into the sub, so I suggest that, once out there, you unscrew the drain plug, let it fill with water and sink to the bottom."

They pulled it back to the beach where Giz passed a piece of folded paper to Mace. When Mace raised his eyebrows Giz said, "It's what you came for isn't it? The co-ordinates? It's important that you return with them."

"Thanks!" said Mace, a knowing smile spreading across his face.

"By the way," cautioned Giz, "if I were you, I wouldn't say a word about meeting any people, if you get what I mean."

"We understand perfectly," said Jordan, gently rubbing a bruise on his head.

"Also, on the way back to your sub you will need to think up a credible story about how you lost your Zodiac. And just one other thing to put your minds at rest: none of us are carriers of Leoenzide. You will not be taking the disease back with you."

The three men stood there in an uneasy silence, and then Mace stepped forward and put out his hand. He went down the line shaking hands with everyone. When he got to Rick, he stopped, and with a smile spreading across his face he said, "You were good, mate! Very, very good! You really had us believing everything you told us." Then, nodding his head toward Mihi he added, "If I were in your shoes, Rick, I'd be applying for permanent residence in this country."

As Mace let go of Giz's hand, Giz turned and pointed to the blood-stained bullet hole through the back of his boot heel. "I've got a memento of your visit," he said.

"Did I do that?" Mace asked in a surprised voice.

"None other."

"Well, Someone was sure looking after you!"

J.B. handed the two automatics, minus their ammunition, to Jordan who put them in the dinghy. He then passed Jordan a can containing their remaining ammunition. "It'll take you a wee while to get that lid off," he told him with a smile.

Mace and Spooner got into the dinghy, and Jordan, with his trouser legs rolled up above his knees, pushed it out to where they could lower the outboard motor clear of the bottom, then climbed aboard. With a single yank on the starter cord the outboard motor burst into life. Mace turned and gave them a snappy salute, and then they were off.

As the group on the beach watched the dinghy getting smaller and smaller, Rick turned to Giz with a furrowed brow, "What were those co-ordinates of, that you gave to Mace?"

"It was the location of some derelict buildings near Henderson. We've been wanting to erect a new seed-raising and potting shed there but weren't sure how to get rid of the old buildings. Not only would it be a good site for them to practice their napalm runs on, the heat will also get rid of the masses of weeds there."

A relieved smile spread across Rick's face.

J.B., watching through binoculars, said, "I think I can see the sub. Yep. It's the sub alright."

After a while Giz said, "Okay. Let's head up to the gold mine for some bullion."

CHAPTER SIX

At the mine, they were surprised to find the safe open and three gold bricks scattered across the floor between two adult skeletons. What had happened was anyone's guess. They put two of the bricks back in the safe, together with a receipt for the one they were taking, then shut the heavy steel door and turned the wheel until it locked with a loud clunk. They then drove half an hour to the macadamia nut plantation where they shared their story with those who had remained behind. Camp had been set up in two houses there, and Spider and Woody had washing drying on a rope strung between two trees.

It was Friday and they decided, by consensus, to stay there until Tuesday morning. The rest of the day was spent in getting ready for the Sabbath. Giz shot a yearling calf, and he and J.B. spit-roasted its hind legs in a corrugated iron lean-to under some large macrocarpa trees. Mihi and Spider set the tables and prepared the ingredients for their evening meal. Rick, helped by Woody, heated water in a forty-four-gallon drum so they all could have a good wash before the Sabbath.

At sunset, everyone and everything was spik and span. The table was loaded with baked kumara, pumpkin and young mamaku shoots, together with a bowl full of the small sweet roasted bulbs of wild onions, and fresh cabbage from young cabbage tree crowns. And there was a large dish of edible fern and puha that Mihi had gathered and steamed, plus the two legs of spit-roasted veal. Bowls of pan-roasted macadamia nuts were spread evenly along the table. At each end of the table was a candle.

When everyone was seated, Mihi lit the first one and said, "This candle is to remind us to remember the Sabbath." As she lit the second one, she said, "This candle is to remind us that Jesus meets with us in a special way on this day."

Spider offered up thanks for the Lord's protection and blessing on their mission, after which he broke a large potato-bread wafer and offered a piece to each person, saying, "The body of the Lord Jesus that was broken for you." He then took a glass of dark red grape juice and held it up, saying, "Jesus said, 'This is my blood of the covenant which is poured out for many for the forgiveness of sins. Drink from it all of you.'" The glass was passed from one to another around the table and they each took a sip.

It was a wonderful meal, finished with a small handful each of roasted macadamia nuts. Rick, with Mihi seated close beside him, could never remember being so content and happy. After they had all eaten their fill, Woody took out his harmonica and they sang rousing songs of the kingdom of God that the Waitak musicians had composed over the two decades since the revival. Some songs were warlike in their intensity, others very devotional and moving.

It had become the custom of the community to go to bed early and get up with the birds, and that night was no different.

The next morning was foggy, but it soon cleared away to a beautiful sunny winter's day. After devotions, Rick asked Mihi if she would like to go for a walk. She rushed off to get her automatic and they set off through the pastures that were rapidly reverting back to bush land. They walked, hand in hand, for about twenty minutes until they came to a stream. There they found a grassy spot on the bank, beside a large totara tree, and sprawled on the ground. Rick lay on his stomach with his head propped in his hands, looking into Mihi's eyes.

"We need a day like this every week, where we can get off the treadmill to focus on relationships . . . especially ours," said Rick.

Mihi sat up. "Look who's preaching now!" she laughed.

"Yeah, I know I have been slow to catch on," he admitted. "Come here."

He rolled onto his back and held up his arms. She sank into them and they kissed tenderly and long.

"Mihi, will you marry me?"

"Oh, Ricky. I love you. I want to be with you for the rest of my life. Of course, I'll marry you!"

"Do you think your dad will marry us?"

"He asked me the other day when we were going to tie the knot."

"Did he? The old rascal."

They kissed again. Rick reached under Mihi's top and cradled one of her breasts in his hand. She gently took his wrist and pushed hand away. "When we get married," she said firmly but kindly.

"Spoil sport," he grinned.

"Come on! Beat you back," she challenged, jumping to her feet. Rick caught her foot, pulled her down and they wrestled playfully on the grass. He was astonished how agile and supple Mihi was. One moment he was holding her down, the next she had squirmed out of his grasp, flipped him on his back and was seated on his chest with her knees on his shoulders. "Fall!" she cried. He reached behind and pinched her bottom. She shot forward with a squeal, leapt to her feet, scooped up her gun and raced off with Rick in hot pursuit.

Mihi ran like the wind, holding her automatic over her head with her right hand to help maintain balance. A pair of quail flew out of the grass at her feet. At the next grove of trees Rick dived for cover and, gasping for breath, crawled into a clump of bracken fern. Mihi, realising that he was no longer following, came looking for him, suspecting that he was hiding from her. As she came near to his hiding place, he struggled to muffle his breathing. Sensing something in the bracken ahead she aimed her automatic at the clump and yelled, "Ricky! Come and help me! I've got a wild pig cornered here in the fern! I need you to help me drag it out after I shoot it!"

Rick leapt to his feet with ashen face, yelling, "Don't shoot! It's me!"

When Mihi doubled up with laughter he fell back gasping, "You nearly gave me a heart attack."

The next day—Sunday—while they were gathering bucket-loads of fallen nuts, Rick asked Spider if he would give his blessing to their marriage. The grey-headed man put down his bucket, turned and looked at Rick with a twinkle in his eye. "You're a fine man, Rick," he said, "and we are honoured to have you with us. I couldn't think of a better husband for Mihi. But what's going to happen to Mihi if you sail off to Australia?"

"I'll take her with me."

"You will?"

"I certainly don't intend to leave her behind."

"Then you have my blessing."

"What would you suggest that I give Mihi as a token of our engagement?"

"Ask the quartermasters to find you a nice ring. There's lots to choose from so you should be able to find one that will fit her finger."

"I'll do that as soon as I return. I have just one other request to make of you. Would you, please, on our behalf, announce our engagement at the meal this evening?"

"I would be honoured and proud to do that, Rick. And I have a request to make of you."

"What's that?"

"When two people get married, they become one flesh. That is true even if they don't have a child, but it is especially true when they do. Both you and Mihi will become one in that child. But that unity will be severely compromised if you and Mihi have different philosophies of life. You understand what I mean, don't you, Rick? You and Mihi can't be truly one if she serves Christ and you don't. And, in spiritual matters, your child will be torn between its allegiance to you and its allegiance to the mother. I don't question your love for Mihi, Rick. I am, however, praying that you will learn to love Jesus even more than you love her. When that happens, I will be at peace because Mihi, and your children, will then have a secure future."

Rick didn't respond, but Spider could see that he was deep in thought. They worked on together, saying nothing more.

That evening, when Spider announced their engagement, there were cheers and clapping. Woody started a jolly tune on his mouth organ and the men got up and danced with each other, taking turns to excuse whoever was dancing with the radiant Mihi.

The next two days were spent loading the nuts into bags for the trip back to Auckland. The motor-cycles, quad bike and ATVs were serviced, and on the final evening they loaded the trailers so they could get a good hour on the road before the first expected flight of the Australian spy plane. J.B. suggested that they return home via the thermal hot pools at Miranda, and everyone seconded it. A relaxing soak in the hot pool would be the icing on their cake.

At Miranda they were disappointed to find that the large pool was polluted with leaf litter and was far too hot to swim in. Having come so far, though, they decided to clean out some of the smaller spas where the water temperature could be controlled. Mihi invited Rick to join her in a spa together with her dad and J.B. As they were getting into the water J.B. turned to Rick and said, "Congratulations, Rick, on winning a wonderful woman. We are all thrilled that you and Mihi plan to get married. You are a fine man and we are happy for Mihi."

"Thanks, J.B. I feel like the cat with the cream."

As they seated themselves around the pool, J.B. continued, "May I ask you a personal question, Rick?"

"Go ahead."

"Do you understand what it means to be marrying a committed Christian?"

"Dad and I have talked about it briefly."

"Why don't you ask the Lord into your life, Rick, then you'd both be of one heart and mind?"

"I've always been a very self-sufficient person, J.B.—master of my own destiny. It wasn't until I came here to Aotearoa that I discovered that was an illusion. In the short time that I have been here I have seen what a belief in God has done for people, and how God cares for those who love and serve him. I want that kind of life-changing relationship too. It's just, well, I'm not sure how to go about it."

Mihi grabbed Spider's hand, "Dad, you help him."

Spider leaned toward Rick. "It's no more difficult than building a relationship with Mihi, Rick. The relationship grows until you get to the point where you decide to make a commitment to each other. You then muster up the courage to ask."

"It's as easy as that?" asked Rick.

"God definitely wants a relationship with you, Rick. There's no question about that. So if you want a relationship with him, what's stopping you? Go ahead and ask. And, just as your relationship with Mihi will be sealed with an engagement ring, so your relationship with God will be sealed with baptism."

Rick didn't respond. He just sat there, deep in thought, staring through a gap in the wall where a decayed plank had fallen out.

"Hey, Rick!" interrupted Spider whose eyes had suddenly lit up. "It has just occurred to me what your grandmother's dream was about."

"What dream was that?" asked J.B.

Rick smiled a weak smile. "My grandmother said she saw me being lowered into a cloud. And through the cloud she could hear angels singing. She wasn't sure what it meant. She thought it might have been about my death. The dream was so vivid she referred to it several times over the years."

The small group looked into each other's eyes momentarily then leapt to their feet, hi-fiving and shouting, "Hallelujah!"

Rick stared at them as though they had gone mad.

Mihi grabbed Rick's hands and pulled him into a standing position. "Ricky," she said with tears in her eyes, "Jesus died to make it possible for you to have God as your best friend. So ask God to be your special friend, just as you asked me."

"Mihi, I really want this relationship. I really do."

"Then for goodness' sake, tell him!"

When Rick seemed to hesitate, she insisted, "Now!"

"Lord," said Rick looking upward, "I really want you in my life. I want you to be my special Friend. I know I'm not worthy to be your friend, but I've learnt that Jesus, through his death on the cross, has made me worthy."

"Rick," said Spider, offering him his hand, "Welcome into God's family. Do you wish to seal that decision by being baptised?"

"I do."

"Wonderful. We will now make your grandmother's dream come true."

"What do you mean?"

"You have just died to Satan's kingdom, so we are going to bury you in an aqueous grave. But don't worry, we will raise you up again, just as God's Spirit is raising you up to a new life in Jesus' kingdom."

J.B. went out and called all the others into their cubicle while Spider explained the significance of baptism to Rick. As soon as they were all in and standing around the wall Spider announced that Rick had given his life to the Lord and wished to be baptised. With Rick standing in front of him in the water, Spider raised his right hand and said, "Rick, because you have accepted Jesus as your Lord and Saviour, it is my privilege and honour to seal that commitment by baptising you in the name of the Father, the Son and the Holy Spirit." Having said that he lowered Rick through a layer of water vapour into the pool then lifted him up out of the water again. Everyone shouted for joy, except Mihi, who was so overwhelmed that she dissolved into tears.

Spider placed his hand on her shoulder and lowered his head to look into her eyes. "You okay, sweetheart?" he asked tenderly.

"Yes, Dad," she sniffed. "I'm just so happy."

"Listen up, everyone," called Spider. "Let's sing the doxology together."

Giz, with his wonderful baritone voice, began, and everyone joined in, singing a cappella:

> *Praise God from whom all blessings flow,*
> *Praise Him all creatures here below,*
> *Praise Him above you heavenly host,*
> *Praise Father, Son and Holy Ghost.*

Years afterward, those who were there claimed that the singing was the most beautiful, powerful and heart-moving they had ever experienced. Some claimed that it was because the heavenly host had been rejoicing with them.

The folk at Waitak settlement were thrilled to hear the good news about Rick's conversion, and his engagement to Mihi, and were eager to hear about the adventures they had on the Coromandel. But then came devastating news for Rick. In the midst of their excited talking, Cardiac Porter coughed loudly, and everyone went silent. He put one hand on Rick's shoulder and told him, as gently as he could, that his escape boat had been destroyed. From the evidence at the site, it seemed that some military personnel had camped in a nearby house for several days—no doubt waiting for the boat builders to return—before they burned the escape boat and left. Mihi put her arm around Rick's waist, but he was too traumatised to respond. He just stood there in shock with a frozen look of hurt on his face.

The next day Mihi came to see how he was.

"I didn't sleep much last night," he confessed. "I think I now understand a little of how you must have felt when you lost your homes, not once, but twice."

"Think of the blessings, Rick," said Mihi. "You hadn't installed Draper's GPS locator or Kelly's wind-powered generator, so you've still got those. Besides, that boat would have been too small for both of us."

Rick smiled. "Ah Mihi, what a blessing and encouragement you are. You have such a beautiful, simple wisdom."

That night at prayer meeting they offered up thanks that the Lord had preserved their lives once again.

The next day Chippy took Rick and Mihi to have a look at the remains of the boat and house. Rick was hoping that he might still be able to salvage the water pumps. The site was just a heap of ash, charred timber and burnt corrugated iron. Rick walked over to where the end of a scorched plank poking out from beneath several sheets of scorched corrugated iron with fresh rust on them. He lifted it to see what was underneath when a powerful explosion hurled him backward down the grassy bank to the footpath below. The blast itself didn't hurt him, apart from making his ears ring for a couple of days, but the rain of rubble that fell on him split his scalp and right cheek bone. Mihi and Chippy were at his side in an instant.

"Don't go near any of that stuff," Rick warned. "It's been booby-trapped."

As Mihi patched him up he said, "Mihi, this makes me all the more determined to escape from Aotearoa to reveal to the world what is happening here. These injustices against innocent people cannot be allowed to continue. And the only way to stop them trying to exterminate us is to prove that their prejudice about people here being carriers of Leoenzide is patently false. We have to build another boat."

"A two-berth boat?"

"Yes, a two-berth boat!"

CHAPTER SEVEN

The next three weeks were spent looking for another boat that they could modify. The best they could find was a laminated double-skinned kauri boat, a few years old, but in very good condition. It was in a cradle at Stillwater, some distance away—too far away, in fact, to work on at its present location. They had to get it much nearer the settlement. When Rick said the best place would be a large building in which they could work on the boat under cover, Woody suggested a large building at Hobsonville, as it was on the edge of the upper Waitemata Harbour and had a slipway nearby. Two sides of the building had been buckled in by the tsunami, but apart from that, it should be eminently suitable for their needs.

Rick, Mihi and Chippy went to inspect the building and were pleased with its potential. The interior needed to be stripped, but with a couple of working-bees they could be ready to start work in a week or two. The Council approved their proposal. It organised a three-day working bee that would involve most able-bodied people from Waitak. The Council also appointed five men: Chippy, Fergus, Smiley, Kelly and Watson, to work with them full time.

Other families were rostered on a weekly basis to bring the workers food. In response to her own request, Mihi was appointed "chief cook and bottle washer" for the boat builders. Giz and J.B. were given the responsibility of working out a security plan for the site plus a contingency plan should they come under attack. At the working bee, a large area was cleared for them to work in; and some compartments along one side were converted into living quarters.

Rick inspected the road between Stillwater and Hobsonville. Many bushes had taken root in the cracks that had opened in the seal of the road. He estimated that with two days' work, four men could remove enough of the larger bushes for them to make a direct and speedy run with the boat after the 'spy in the sky' plane had passed over.

He sent Fergus, Chippie, Smiley and Kelly to prepare the route while he and Watson went out to find a large boat hauler. The Quartermaster's Store had given them two addresses to check out. They chose the better of the two haulers, did a quick service on it and drove it to Hobsonville where they parked it inside the large building so they could give it a much more thorough servicing. It would be a disaster if it broke down on the road with the boat on it.

Watson and Horse spent a whole day going over the truck, draining, flushing and refilling the engine with new oil, replacing the old oil and air filters with new ones, re-setting the timing, and checking the hydraulics. When they had finished, the engine was purring. Finally, they fitted new tyres all round.

Rick decided he wouldn't take the boat-hauler to Stillwater until they were ready to load the boat on it. Leaving Watson and Kelly behind with instructions to bring the boat hauler through in forty-eight hours, he departed with the others. At Stillwater, they immediately set about creating a track for the boat hauler to reverse down to the lower side of the cradle that held the chosen vessel. Chippy built a makeshift slipway so they could skid the boat onto the deck of the hauler from its cradle. Rick calculated that they may not have time to load, block and strap the boat into place between flights of the spy plane.

They were in the process of putting the finishing touches to the cradle when they heard the truck's horn blaring from the road up the hill. Woody rushed to show them the way down. He told Watson to park the hauler under some huge macrocarpa trees at the end of the road until they were given the all-clear by Joshua, whose job was to keep tabs on the flights of the spy plane and give them an 'all-clear' as soon as the plane had passed overhead.

Getting the boat onto the hauler without the help of a crane was much more difficult than they had anticipated. It took two hours of jacking and manoeuvring with ropes and pullies to get it repositioned and secured on the hauler's deck. Watson drove back to the shelter of the macrocarpas until the next "window." After a couple of adjustments to their precious load, with shouts of triumph, they drove back to Hobsonville. Heavy overcast skies and occasional downpours gave them extra protection from surveillance by the Aussie plane. The journey home was without incident, thanks to the good work the team had done in clearing a track along the highway. The shrubs, which had been more than a metre high, had been cut off level with the road so that no sharp stumps remained to pierce the tyres.

Back inside the large building at Hobsonville, they left the yacht on the trailer and built a platform around it from which they could work. The big shed was ideal for their purpose as the vast airspace inside would dissipate any heat produced by their generator. Mihi, who wanted to keep everyone motivated, gave the name of 'Launch Bay' to the place where their completed boat would enter the water.

— o —

Rick and Mihi decided to get married early in August. The whole Waitak settlement was throbbing with excitement. The church, decorated with fresh ponga fronds and flowers, had never looked as beautiful as it did that Sunday morning when they exchanged vows. Several families from the Keri Keri settlement came to the wedding. Rick was dressed in new soft leather trousers and waistcoat—presents from the Keri Keri group—and Mihi chose a beautiful traditional flax skirt that hung below her knees. It was dyed in traditional colours and was encircled with white pois around the waist. She wore a soft woven top that accentuated her womanhood, and carried a simple bunch of white flowers tied with a piece of coloured flax. She was so ravishingly beautiful that her appearance on the arm of her father brought gasps of admiration from everyone. Rick wanted to rush and gather her in his arms.

It was a proud day for Spider. With tears running down his cheeks, he escorted his daughter into church, handed her over to the groom, and then moved to the front to conduct the wedding service.

There were dishes of food at the wedding celebration that people hadn't seen for years. Bottles of the best non-alchoholic wines, reserved for occasions such as this, were on the tables. Folk had made a special effort to put on a meal that would not be forgotten. They knew, deep down, that Rick and Mihi would soon be taking a huge risk for them all, and that they could be sailing away to never be seen or heard of again. While there was lots of laughter, mingled with the happiness were also many tears. In his speech, Rick said that they had chosen late January to early February as the time they would set sail, and that it would be their honeymoon trip. Mihi gave Rick a leather-bound Bible, and he presented her with a beautiful greenstone pendant.

Two weeks earlier, Horse had moved out of his cottage and in with Woody, so that his home could be prepared for Rick and Mihi. He said, tongue-in-cheek, that he didn't mind because after they had gone, he would get it back with all the trimmings. The village ladies repainted the interior and spruced it up for the couple. A double bed replaced the bunks and was covered with a beautiful hand-made quilt from the Keri Keri group. Mihi determined that this quilt was one of the treasures she would take with her on their boat.

It was decided to stick with the original plan for the boat, with the exception that it would now be fitted for a crew of two, rather than just one. By October, the boat had been closed in and painted a flat grey-green colour. Two simple sails were made for it; one sail was a grey-black, for sailing at night, and the other was a grey-green for use by day. The upper deck was painted with grey-green paint that had black sand spread over it while still wet, to provide a good non-slip surface. Every time they were tempted to put something metal on the boat, they held a meeting to discuss every possible alternative. Anything that could reduce radar detection, sonar, and heat reflection was considered and tried. Pullies of Matai wood, made on a lathe, were tested, with the Mark 3 version being chosen for their boat.

By early summer, the boat's interior was nearing completion. Rick had been pondering a name for the vessel and finally settled on *Wakamihi*, "Mihi's boat." The name received instant approval from the community. A new set of maps had been provided and Draper's GPS, and the wind-powered generator were installed. While Mihi had shown herself to be adept at handling a dinghy, she knew nothing about sailing, so Rick decided to spend a couple of months fine-tuning the boat on the inner harbour at night and on overcast days and, at the same time, teaching her how to sail.

Now that the boat was finished, the platform around the hauler was dismantled. The following Wednesday morning, just before sunrise, they jacked open the buckled doors of the shed and backed the *Wakamihi* down the slipway into the rising tide. She lifted off easily, and the hauler was returned to the construction building.

Rick admitted that sailing a boat which had only a few centimetres of freeboard and no handrail would not be easy. *Wakamihi* was, at first, inclined to bury her bow in a rough sea and stall, but he fixed that by an internal adjustment of the ballast and the angle of the mast.

After a particularly frustrating day on the water, Rick decided to go ahead with his original plan to make and install a periscope. He got Horse to help him make one out of strong dark-grey plastic piping and mirrors. Initially, he wanted a periscope that he could raise and lower, but they were unable to get a satisfactory watertight joint on a trial model, so ended up making one that was fixed vertically, but which could be swivelled around three hundred and sixty degrees. Once it was fitted on the front of the boat, it considerably lessened the number of times he had to go up topsides.

Watson wasn't too sure about the periscope, not knowing if the surface of the mirror could expose their position by reflecting light or radar beams. While Rick agreed with him, he concluded that the advantages it offered far outweighed the risk.

Mihi was a willing student and was quick to learn. Teaching her to sail from below decks was Rick's most difficult assignment. While she was full of confidence up on deck, down below, sailing with her eyes fixed to the periscope with occasional glances to the compass and GPS, was a different story. However, after several weeks of training in back waters for ten hours a day, she eventually became a proficient and confident sailor. At the end of each day the boat was anchored under trees growing along the bank, where they expected it would be concealed from the spy plane.

A week before their planned departure they filled the cupboards with stocks of cheeses and preserves, and other suitable foods. All the charts and instruments were in place, and the water tanks were flushed out and refilled. At a ceremony on Sunday morning, Cardiac Porter presented Rick and Mihi with a small, carved puriri chest containing gold ingots in leather bags. Watson and Horse had made the mould for them, and each ingot was stamped with the community's emblem of a cross and a dove surrounded by the radiance of the Shekinah glory. Cardiac told them that gold was a universal currency, so no matter what country they went to they would be able to cover their costs.

CHAPTER EIGHT

On Friday morning, Rick and Mihi took the fully provisioned yacht out for final sail. Satisfied with its performance, they anchored it and drove back to Swanson where they caught the train to Waitak.

That Sabbath was a mixture of happiness and sadness. Rick and Mihi sat together in church with their arms around each other, while Spider presented an inspiring study from the Bible on never giving in to difficulties but fighting the good fight right to the finish. That evening they all celebrated with a square dance in the community building.

On Sunday morning, Rick told Cardiac that he wanted to shift the *Wakamihi* to Lucas Creek, away from where it could be seen from the road. Cardiac ruminated, then agreed on the condition that he took Mihi and Carla with him. He made it clear, however, that their mission was to shift the yacht to its new anchorage and return immediately to Waitak. Rick and Mihi decided to take a quad bike, and Carla would accompany them on a cross-country motorcycle.

Rick was relieved to see the boat in its usual spot. He told the others that he would sail up the harbour, past Herald Island, and anchor the boat in deep water near the entrance to Lucas Creek. He would then find himself a dinghy to row back to Herald Island wharf. He asked Carla and Mihi to meet him there.

Herald Island, shaped like a sausage, was about a kilometre long and two hundred and fifty metres wide, and was connected to the mainland by a causeway. After bedding in the anchor, Rick hauled a couple of dead branches onto the *Wakamihi* and hoped that from the shore it would look derelict and partly submerged. When he got to the wharf, Mihi and Carla met him with concern written all over their faces. They told him they had heard vehicles driving down the Whenuapai Airfield.

Early next morning, J.B., and Giz came to join them. They were anxious because it appeared that the Australian military had stepped up their surveillance. Sure enough, not long after their arrival, a vehicle drove onto the far end of the causeway leading to Herald Island. On seeing armed people in the distance, two men stopped the vehicle suddenly, opened the doors and jumped out. One waved a towel back and forth over his head.

In response, Giz took off his shirt, stepped into the middle of the road and did the same. One of the men, holding a white cloth over his head, then came towards them on foot.

"Who are you and what do you want?" Giz asked him bluntly.

"I'm Trueson. We're 'naki people from down south," said the stranger.

"Why have you come up here?" asked Giz.

"The mountain erupted and covered our farmland land with ash so we were forced to move out."

"How did you survive the plague?"

"All of us, that is, eight families, lived in a remote valley, and shortly before the plague struck, a major landslide caused by two weeks of heavy rain cut us off from the outside world. Council engineers examined the road and decided that the expense of repairing it wasn't warranted and that another route would have to be cut into the valley. We had to dry off our cows, and supplies were flown in to us by top-dresser aircraft. Then came the plague. We heard about it on the news, and when we talked to people on the phone, they told us we were in the best place in Aotearoa and that we should stay put. We didn't move out of that valley for three months. We'd still be back there if it wasn't for Mount Taranaki blowing its top. That's why we have come north."

"How many of you are there?"

"Eleven men, plus women and kids. The others are in houses at the other end of the airfield."

"Have you got enough food for at least two days?"

"Yes. We're well stocked with provisions."

"I haven't got time now to tell you what a perilous situation we are in, but here's what I would like you to do. Go back to your vehicle and tell the others to return to their families, and keep out of sight for the next few days. Their lives may depend on that. Do you understand?"

"No, but we'll do as you ask. This is your turf."

"Good. Just briefly, ravening dogs are not our problem here in Auckland. Our enemy is the Australian military. They are out to exterminate us. I would like you, as a representative of your group, to stay with me, at least for the next day or two. Will you do that?"

"I've got heaps of questions, but yes."

"Okay, come back to me as soon as you have delivered the message. Don't delay because we're in for a rough night, weather-wise," Giz said, looking up at the cirrus clouds sweeping in from the west like the raised tails of a herd of stampeding horses.

"Not a good sign," agreed Trueson as he moved off.

When Trueson returned, Giz told Carla to take him into a nearby house he had chosen as a temporary HQ, and to get him to make a list of all the people who had come with him. When Giz came indoors she handed him a list of eleven males.

"Look at this," Carla said to J.B., pointing to one of the names. "Ari. That's uncommon. I would never have expected to have found another person with that name."

"You mean . . .?"

"Could be," she said nodding her head.

They went into the dining room and found Trueson sitting at a table, his face illuminated by the weak glow of an old kerosene lamp.

"Thanks for the list of names," said J.B. as he slid into a chair.

A sudden rain squall battered the western side of the house, rattling the windows and the loose corrugated iron on the roof. The sharpness of the beating rain indicated that there was sleet in it. There was a crashing and banging outside as an empty forty-four-gallon drum, toppled by the wind, clattered across the road. After a brief lull, the wind picked up and blew with a greater fury. The darkness of the night accentuated every sound, especially the low frequency humming of the wildly swaying power(less) wires and the tree branches thrashing against the house.

"Tell me about this person," shouted J.B. to Trueson, pointing to Ari's name on the list.

"What do you want to know?"

"We've got all night, so start at the beginning."

"Well, we don't have to go too far back. He's not really one of us. What I mean is, he didn't come from our valley."

J.B. and Carla glanced at each other with raised eyebrows.

CHAPTER NINE

Just then Watson entered. When he saw the stranger, he beckoned J.B. into the hallway. "Bad news, I'm afraid. We got in touch with Cardiac. He said a large drone flew down the valley below the Waitak dam late this afternoon. It appeared to be taking a good look beneath the trees at our cabins there. After it had departed, Cardiac got everyone out on the train to Swanson and told them to scatter. He has stayed behind to man the radio."

Carla pulled up a chair and sat down at the table with Trueson. "If Ari isn't a Taranaki man, how and when did he join up with you?" she asked. Trueson replied, "About twenty-five years ago, five men from our valley decided to go up to Hamilton on a recce to see if anyone else had survived the plague. They were parked on the side of the main road eating their lunch when they heard a motorbike coming. They stepped out onto the road and waved the fellow down.

"When he stopped, they asked him lots of questions but the only thing he could remember clearly was his name. At that time, he didn't know where he had come from or even where he was going. From the heavy bruising on his forehead, it appeared that he had had an accident and hurt himself quite badly. We assumed he was suffering from trauma-induced amnesia. He did recover some childhood memories early on, and bit by bit other memories are coming back to him. He settled in with us and has proved himself to be an honest, unselfish man and a great worker."

When he had finished speaking, he looked closely at Carla and asked, "Do you know this man?"

"Yes, we know him. He went missing on a trip from Whangarei to Auckland twenty-five years ago. He was thirty years old then, so that would make him fifty-five now."

"Yes, that'd be right."

"I wonder if he will recognise any of us?"

"During the night the gale blew itself out. Early next morning, half an hour before dawn, J.B. sent a six-man foot patrol along Herald Island towards the wharf to check the houses to see how many people were still on the island and what condition they were in.

"They were in the process of doing this when a large troop-carrying chopper with twin rotors came thundering in from the east. It circled over the water and landed on the northern side at Christmas Beach. Troops jumped out of the chopper, six of whom were detailed to seal off the exit from the island via the causeway. The rest were double-marched to the opposite end of the island where they went systematically from house to house, firing tear-gas grenades through the windows and waiting with their automatics ready for anyone who might try to escape. It soon became obvious to them that the island's residents were long gone.

About ten minutes into the operation, a large drone that had arrived with the chopper peeled away from the island and began flying slowly around each one at roof-top level, inspecting the houses at the other end of the causeway. "Blast!" muttered J.B. "We've got two quad bikes parked outside under the trees. And their wheel tracks will still be fresh in the grass. Looks like we're caught this time with no escape exit."

At Giz's suggestion, Carla and Mihi opened the sliding door to the second-floor balcony and waited with their guns at the ready. As soon as the drone was level with them, they fired a salvo of shots into it sending it into a steep side-slip. It struck one of the quad-bikes, splitting its fuel tank, which erupted in a sheet of flame against the house.

"Everybody out!" yelled J.B.

They all raced across the Terrace and took shelter in the old fire station at Kowhai beach. Giz sent two men out to see what the Aussies were doing. They returned with the disturbing news that they were being sandwiched between the troops guarding the causeway and the troops coming toward them from the other end of the island.

"Okay," said Giz. "I don't feel at all good about this. I don't like the idea of having to kill others in order to save our own skins." After a pause he added, "There has to be a better way. I'd be grateful, Fergus, if you would ask the Lord, on behalf of all of us here, to help us make wise decisions in this difficult situation."

"You surely don't believe that a prayer is going to help you?" asked one of the Taranaki men sarcastically.

"Do you have any better suggestions?" snapped Woody.

The objector looked at him blankly, then shrugged his shoulders.

"Okay, Fergus," said Woody.

"Lord, as you know, we are in a bit of a fix here. You've helped us before. Please help us again. We need to find a way out of this trap without taking anyone's life, or losing our own, we ask in Jesus' name," prayed Fergus simply.

"Amen," responded the men from Waitak.

"Right. Let's go," Woody said, leading off at a trot down Ferry Parade. On the way they wondered about the fire and smoke rolling upwards from the house that J.B. had been using as his headquarters. When they came to Coleman Street, they cut through the backs of the houses to a point where they were able to spy on the six on-duty soldiers without being seen. Providentially, the soldiers were all watching the burning building with their backs to Woody's group. The officer in charge was talking on a small radio transceiver. After switching off, he spoke to his men and three of them set off across the causeway at the double.

Woody waited until they were two hundred metres away. He then asked three of his men to keep their guns trained on the remaining guards, and split the rest into two groups. One group approached the troops from behind the houses on the southern side of the entrance to the causeway, the other from behind the houses on the northern side.

At a signal from Woody the three groups simultaneously stepped into the open and called upon the soldiers to lay down their weapons. The Aussies were taken completely by surprise. At first they hesitated, but when they realised they were out-gunned, they soon obeyed. Woody moved in and kicked their weapons over the side into the sea. He then marched them down the causeway.

At the other end of the causeway, J.B. was in the process of getting everyone out of the area when it was reported to him that three armed soldiers were coming across at the double. He ordered Carla, Rick and Mihi to follow him, and rushed to the road. When the soldiers saw them, they leapt through the trees that lined the causeway. But because the tide was high, they had next to no cover.

As soon as Woody's group got close enough, J.B. called upon the soldiers to surrender. When there was no response after his second call he stepped to the side of the road and angled a burst of automatic fire over their heads. Woody followed up with a burst from his end. One of the trapped soldiers then raised a handkerchief over his head. "Leave your guns on the road and stand up with your hands on your heads," J.B. yelled. Woody's squad moved in, picked up their weapons and tossed them into the sea, then brought the six prisoners to J.B.

At that point, J.B. noticed Ari. Although he was much older, there was no doubt that it was the Ari he had known years ago. He went to him and said, "Hello, Ari. Do you remember me?" Ari looked blank. After a moment's reflection he replied, "I don't know who you are, but I have the feeling we have met before. Your face looks familiar."

"I'm J.B."

"J.B." said Ari reflectively. Then his eyes lit up and he stepped forward and gave J.B. a big hug. "Ah, J.B. it's so good to meet you again. It's been a long time."

Then J.B. turned to the captive group and, speaking in Maori, he said to his team, "We've got to get as far away from here as we can, as quickly as we can. We'll keep the prisoners in case we need hostages. We don't have any vehicles, so we'll have to hoof it, but that could be to our advantage as there won't be any vehicle noises to give away our position. We'll take the road to the north of the Whenuapai Airfield. With luck, we will be six kilometres away from here in less than an hour."

Turning to the prisoners J.B. said in English, "You six get out in front and keep together." Then, winking to Rick and Mihi, he added in a voice that the soldiers would hear, "Should they get difficult or attempt to escape, don't muck around, just shoot them." Then in a louder voice, "Okay. Let's move off at double quick time!"

Once they got moving Rick came up alongside J.B. and asked quietly, "What do you intend doing with the prisoners once we get out of here?"

"I don't know yet, but I'll think of something."

After fifteen minutes of jogging, J.B. called a halt to give everyone a breather. They were just getting to their feet again when they heard the big chopper on Herald Island start up. J.B. spoke in Maori, "Once it gets up into the air we will need to get out of sight, so keep your eyes peeled for a good cover with an escape route." Then, in English he said, "Okay, everyone. Let's go!"

They hadn't been on the road more than two minutes when they heard the revs on the chopper increase to maximum as it lifted off. "Which way do you think it's going?" Rick asked J.B.

"Can't tell just yet. Everyone halt!"

They stood there listening, noticing that the chopper was moving away from them.

"That's a relief," said Rick.

"Hey!" yelled Ari. "One of the prisoners has got an R.T."

J.B. swung around to see four prisoners standing close together shielding the one with the radio transceiver from the sight of their captors. J.B. fired a shot over their heads and they dropped to the road. He marched up to the prisoners and said, "I warned you that if there was any trouble, we'd shoot you. Obviously you didn't think I was serious. You!" J.B. said, indicating the man with the radio transceiver in his hand, "stand up and take your clothes off."

The soldier sneered, but leapt to his feet when J.B. fired a bullet into the road beside him, spraying him with stone chips. While he was removing his clothes, J.B. told Carla that she was in charge until he got back. He told her to get all the prisoners to strip off everything, including their underclothes.

Everything that wasn't clothing, including watches, was to be confiscated, and the clothing returned to the men to be put back on. Turning to Kelly and Trueson he said. "Come with me." Out of earshot of the others he said, "Kelly, I want you to give your quad bike to the four Taranaki men." Then to Trueson, "Two of you can get on the bike and two can crouch in the trailer. I want you fellows to get back to the other Taranaki folk if possible, then go to ground until the trouble has passed. Once things have quietened down, using all caution, I want you to get all the people into the manuka thicket by the creek at the end of Dale Road, which is off Totara Road." With a stick he drew a sketch of the route on the ground as he spoke. "We'll meet you here," he said, stabbing the spot with his stick. "If we don't make it, take the people across the creek after dark, and back to the Swanson area. Our group is too big as it is, so both your and our chances of escaping will be better if we split up."

Back with the group J.B. called, "Rick. Take this pistol and come with me please." The two men led the prisoner away. They entered a property and took the prisoner around the back of the house and into a large double garage with a truck parked inside. J.B. took out a pair of handcuffs and addressed the prisoner: "For me, killing is an evil. But if I have to choose between the two evils of killing you or having my people killed, then I'll choose the lesser of the two evils. However, if you co-operate you will save your own skin. Now get into the truck. Rick, go around the other side, open the door and keep him covered."

J.B. then handcuffed the prisoner to the steering wheel. "If you get out of this truck and wild dogs get you, you'll either be eaten on the spot or you'll die from Leoenzide within a week. I recommend, therefore, that you stay put. As soon as we get out of this mess someone will come back and free you. I'm taking this with me," he added, removing the prisoner's ID tag. Looking at it and added, "So your name is Carson. Well, Carson, for your sake I hope we won't have to meet again." He then locked the prisoner inside the cab.

By the time J.B. and Rick returned to the others, the Taranaki group was already out of sight around the bend of the road. Rick noticed that everyone was looking decidedly uncomfortable. The Waitak people were upset because they thought that J.B. had executed the man, and the smirks had disappeared from the other prisoners' faces. Capitalising on their discomfort, J.B. said to the prisoners, "Desperate times demand desperate measures. We didn't attack you. We have been living here in peace but you came to attack and kill us. Well, we are not going to put up with it. We'd be perfectly justified in shooting all of you right here and now. In fact, we'd be better off if we did, as your presence with us handicaps our movement and makes our concealment more difficult. Now take off your I.D. tags and throw them to me."

He pocketed the discarded tags, then got everyone moving again.

Rick speaking quietly to Mihi said, "I doubt that the soldier with the radio got enough message through to reveal where we are, because there is no movement of the chopper in our direction." He had hardly finished when they heard the chopper coming.

"Back into that house everyone!" shouted J.B.

They had just got all the prisoners lying on the floor of the sitting room in a windowless corner, when the big chopper came thundering over the house. But it didn't stop. It kept flying.

"I would say they don't really know where we are," commented Kelly, "but it appears they got a direction on Carson's call. I suspect they will be back."

They heard the chopper fly across the estuary then return. Mihi, who was looking out the laundry window, saw black smoke rising from just outside the shed door and Carson, running back and forth with broken handcuffs dangling from his wrists.

"J.B!" she yelled. "You'd better come and see this."

J.B. came running. One look and he smashed the window with a couple of jabs of his rifle butt, and placed a shot into the ground in front of the soldier's feet. He then yelled out, "Carson, if you're not back inside the shed in three seconds, I'll put the next one in your head! One…two… three!" Carson was gone, but the thick black smoke was still there.

The chopper circled the house and Rick guessed that Carson, now out of sight of those in the house, was probably waving to the chopper from just inside the open shed door. To make sure the soldier didn't get too bold, J.B. fired a bullet through the galvanised wall above where Carson's head would have been. The chopper backed off about one hundred metres and hung there for over a minute. The crew may have assumed it was a trick and weren't prepared to take a risk. A short while later, six soldiers rappelled down to the ground from the chopper, separated into two groups, and approached the house from two different angles.

J.B. took the prisoner's radio out of his pocket and turned it on. "Do you read me?" he asked.

"Is that you, Corporal Carson?" came the reply.

"No, this is not Corporal Carson. My name is J.B. Corporal Carson and his men are in our custody. I want you to call off your troops and send a negotiator to speak with me on the road outside the house where the smoke is coming from."

There was a long pause. The troops stopped their approach and retreated.

J.B. turned to Woody, "Take Watson with you and bring Carson back into the house."

Soon an officer came down the road with a flag. J.B. went out to meet him. The others could see J.B. showing the officer the prisoners' I.D. tags. There was a discussion that lasted about five minutes. At its conclusion the officer stepped back, saluted and returned to his men. After they had all boarded the chopper, it took off and flew across the estuary and up to a high point in Beach Haven that overlooked the upper harbour.

J.B. came indoors and told everyone that he had made a bargain with the military. He would let them have their men back by the end of the day as long as they kept out of the way. The officer wanted some kind of guarantee that J.B. would keep his word, but J.B. told him that he would just have to trust him.

By now it was getting late in the day and everyone was beginning to experience pangs of hunger, having not eaten since early morning. J.B. stood with his chin in his cupped hand, deep in thought. After a few moments of contemplation he said, "Rick and Mihi, come out the back with me."

Outside he asked in a subdued voice, "How soon can you sail?"

"We could leave immediately," they said together.

"Except that we haven't said goodbye to anyone," added Mihi.

"You've heard what happened at Waitak, so there's no point returning there. And we haven't finished the battle with these troops. They are professional soldiers and they are not going to leave thinking that a bunch of civilians has bested them. Furthermore, they know there's really only one way out of here for us, so they won't have far to look after they pick up their men. I think it best that you get away immediately, under cover of dark. Can you drift down the harbour on the outgoing tide?"

"It's too risky," said Rick. "There's no wind, so we can't use a sail. And without a sail or a motor there's nothing to stop us going aground."

"Well, anyway, you two should split off from the rest of us. I suggest you find some way of getting over the estuary and getting back to your boat from the other side. Stay hidden until it is the right time to leave."

"What are you going to do?" asked Mihi.

"We'll take the prisoners to Brigham Creek Road. At the junction I'll release them and tell them to return to this house where they will find their R.T. in the letterbox. As soon as they are out of sight we'll double back and go down Dale Road to meet up with the Taranaki people. I suggest you two stay hidden until we are around the bend in the road. Hopefully the prisoners won't notice your absence. I'll say goodbye to you now and wish you the best of luck. By God's grace we will see you again in the not-too-distant future."

Their hugging was interrupted by yells from inside the house. There was a gunshot. The back door burst open and Watson stumbled out followed by Woody.

"What happened in there, Woody?" asked J.B. in a commanding voice.

"One of the prisoners grabbed Smiley and has got him in the bathroom. He's got Smiley's gun too. It went off in the scuffle."

Furious, J.B. ran to the house. He signalled everyone to move out and ordered Watson to get them moving. "If I don't catch up with you before you get to Brigham Creek Road, release the prisoners just before you get there and tell them to return to this house, and that their radio will be waiting for them in the letterbox. Carla, you stay with me. I need your help."

The group moved off but nobody seemed to notice that Ari had remained behind with Rick and Mihi.

"I'm going to burn the house down, Carla," said J.B.

"That's crazy, boss!"

"No, it's not. As long as Carson has got Smiley in there, he can negotiate with us. He'll probably demand his R.T., and shoot a toe off Smiley every thirty seconds until he gets it. Or something like that. Well, I'm not going to negotiate with him."

"But you could end up burning Smiley to death."

"It's a risk I'm prepared to take, but I seriously doubt it. Carson won't stay there to be incinerated, and I'm gambling that he won't come out without a hostage lest we shoot him. I'll light the fire at the back so he'll have to come out the front. And we'll be waiting there for him. That's why I chose you, Carla, because you are the best shot, and the coolest. Now go and hide yourself in a good spot where you can cover the front door. This time you may have to shoot to maim. Okay?"

"I don't like it, J.B. I don't like it," complained Carla.

"There may be no alternative. Off you go!"

J.B. went to the shed to look for some fuel. He was surprised to see Ari there with Rick and Mihi.

"Ari!" he exclaimed. "Why aren't you with the others?"

Nodding towards Mihi, Ari replied, "Spider's daughter has just told me that she and her husband are going to try to get away from Aotearoa to let the rest of the world know what is happening here. I want to help them get away. Spider would want me to do that. I've decided I'm going to stick with them until they are safely on their way."

J.B. was so focused on what he was looking for that he seemed not to hear.

"This looks like it," he said, sweeping a heap of junk off a drum at the back of the shed. He unscrewed the bung and sniffed. "Diesel," he muttered.

He told the three what he intended doing. Rick gave him a hand to tip some diesel into a bucket. J.B. took it and poured it all along the lower back wall of the house. He then wound some sacking around a broom handle, tied it in place with a short length of copper wire, and dipped it into the petrol tank of the lawnmower. He lit it and set fire to the diesel. After waiting until the back of the house was well alight, he moved to the front to take up a position near Carla.

The old, tinder-dry house burned rapidly.

As Ari, Rick and Mihi watched the fire flaming up the back of the house, suddenly, through the flames and smoke at the rear, charged two men covered in steaming blankets that were on fire in places. The surprise was complete. Before they could react, they were all Carson's hostages. Mihi berated herself silently for having left her gun propped against a wall inside the shed.

"Into the shed, all of you!" demanded Carson as he slapped at his smouldering hair with his free hand. A concrete pit down the centre was covered with planks stained black with oil and grease. Stacked along the one wall was a gearbox, a couple of differentials and piles of other junk. Mihi could see her gun leaning against the wall next to an old lawnmower. She hoped the soldier wouldn't notice it among everything else.

Ari stepped up beside Mihi and said in a low voice, without looking at her, "I'm going to distract him long enough for you to get your rifle and do what you have to do."

"No! Ari, no!" she said firmly.

"I've made up my mind," he replied grimly.

"Shut up, you two! Move to the back of the shed, all of you," demanded Carson. "And put your hands in the air where I can see them."

Ari slipped a shoe off his foot, then stooped down to retrieve it.

"You!" shouted the soldier, stepping towards him. "Get over there with the others!"

Ari, still crouching, twisted around and sprang past Carson, racing for the door. The soldier turned and fired a short burst from the hip and Ari crumpled in a heap.

"Let that be all!" shouted Carson as he turned back to the others. But he never got his sentence finished. A single shot from Mihi hit him in the centre of his chest. His legs buckled, his gun clattered on the concrete and he sank to the floor with a look of utter surprise on his face.

Smiley ran to Ari and checked his pulse, but he was gone. Mihi's gun fell from her hands and she burst into tears in Rick's arms as J.B. and Carla came sprinting through the door. Smiley told them what had happened.

J.B. stepped up to Mihi and squeezed her arm. "What you did, Mihi, was a very brave thing. Had you not stopped this man, many innocent people might have died. You are a true heroine. God rest, dear Ari. He's a martyr in the truest sense of the word. But look, we've got to get out of here pronto. Rick and Mihi, this is an awful time for us to separate, but both of you must take off to the estuary now! Stay hidden and get yourselves over to the other side after dark. God speed and God bless. We'll be praying around the clock for you both."

They hugged again. Before releasing Mihi from his arms, J.B. prayed, "Lord, please take care of this couple. Send strong angels to look after them. Please, Lord, please take them safely to their destination, in Jesus' name I pray. Amen."

"Now get moving!" he said, "Every minute counts."

"What about Ari and Carson?" asked Rick.

"We'll cremate Ari in the house-fire so the dogs don't get him. Lord willing, we shall return and erect a monument to his name on this spot. We'll find some pepper and cover Carson with it to keep the dogs off and, after wrapping him in canvas, we'll leave him by the letterbox. Hopefully the military will return him to his folks in Australia. Now off you go!"

As they parted J.B. called after them, "God speed. We love you!"

CHAPTER TEN

In the trees where Waimarie Road came to an end at the harbour's edge Rick turned to Mihi, whose eyes were red with weeping. He took her in his arms and held her close, not speaking. When he released her, he said, "Well, sweetheart, we are on our own now. For the sake of everyone else we can't afford to take any unnecessary risks. We will lie low until conditions are right for us to take our yacht down the harbour. I'd feel much safer, however, on the other side of the estuary, opposite our boat. The bush is much denser over there. Once we're there, I could slip out to the yacht after dark to get some food."

"Shouldn't we go and live on the yacht?" Mihi sniffed. "It would be more comfortable."

"No. We need find a waterproof house up on the hill on the other side so we can keep an eye on the estuary and the weather. Once we are convinced we have a reasonable chance of getting away, we'll board the yacht and move down the harbour under cover of darkness. But right now, we need to find some way of getting over there." They found a fibreglass dinghy under one of the houses, but the oars were worm-eaten and useless. After rattling around they found a treated plank which they broke in half to use as paddles. The dinghy was light enough for the two of them to carry to the water.

They had to wait until nine-thirty at night before the tide was high enough for them to move off without leaving any footprints in the mud. They paddled the dinghy directly out from the shore so the incoming tide would move them up the estuary to the nearest spit of land on the other side. Paddling a dinghy wasn't easy, but they quickly got into a rhythm that kept it on a steady course. After beaching, they pulled it up the bank and hid it among some bulrushes. They then began their long walk back to a spot opposite the mouth of Lucas Creek.

Their journey through the bush bordering the estuary was difficult and slow in the intensifying darkness. When they got to a point opposite the Wakamihi, Rick swam out to the boat and got some food, soap, a towel and a pair of binoculars that he put in a large black plastic rubbish bag. He blew the bag up with his mouth, tied it off, and towed it back to shore. They found a tile-roofed house on the hillside overlooking the harbour. It had a large concrete tank at the back full of rain-water from the house roof.

Mihi cleaned the bath and Rick filled it. They stood in the bath while they lathered up, and then poured water over each other to rinse off the suds.

As each of the bedrooms contained human skeletons in perished bedding, they wrapped themselves in blankets and a duvet from cupboard in the hallway, and went to sleep on the carpeted floor of the lounge. It was after one o'clock the next afternoon before they awoke. Rick noticed that Mihi's eyes were red and swollen from weeping. He felt bad that he had slept right through, unaware of her grief and without offering her any comfort.

"Blast!" said Rick when he looked at his watch.

"What's the matter?" sniffed Mihi.

"J.B. said he would call at midday."

"Why don't you call him?"

"He warned against it. Said my transmission could be tracked."

"Well, his could too, for that matter."

"True. But he would transmit from a place that he would get away from in a hurry. He said I was to answer with two clicks for yes and one for no. That kind of transmission would be too short to get a proper fix on."

"What's the time for the next transmission?"

"He didn't say. We can't afford to leave the radio on permanently, otherwise we'll run the batteries flat, so we'll listen in on the hour, every hour until we hear from him."

It was noon the next day before they got a call from J.B.

"J.B. calling R&M. Do you receive me?"

Click, click.

"Are you okay?"

Click, click.

"We all got away without any major problems. Out on the Great South Road we heard some gunshots ahead of us so back-tracked and took another route. The next day, young Flip, a Taranki lad who has attached himself to my group, volunteered to go and check it out. When he returned, he told us he found a number of wild dogs that had been shot. Apparently some soldiers had set up an ambush for us, but when these dogs had turned up the soldiers panicked and shot them, thus revealing their position."

There was a pause before J.B. continued: "Waitak is gone and Cardiac is missing. I don't need to say any more. The barometer is dropping again. Looks like we're in for some really murky stuff. Sabbath could be quite nasty, weather-wise. Well, that's it from me. God bless you both. We love you heaps. Over and out."

Rick and Mihi sat there feeling very, very lonely, and traumatised at the loss of Waitak and the probable death of Cardiac.

"I guess if Cardiac is dead, then J.B. will become the natural leader," said Mihi. "He's a good man and loves the Lord."

"He never said anything about Giz. He must have got away."

"Guess we'll never know."

"Don't talk like that!" berated Rick. "We are going to get out of here and return."

"You are a lot more positive about that than I am."

"Mihi, here on dry land, you are trumps. But on the ocean, I'm in my element. Trust me, we will make it. Our boat is an absolute marvel of invisibility to both man and electronic surveillance."

After a pause Rick said, "I doubt that your people will go back into a settlement situation again. It's too risky."

"I doubt it too. Their trust is in us now. And I bet the 'naki people move away in a hurry, now that they've had a taste of the Australian military. I wonder why the spy planes never picked up their settlement in Taranaki?"

"Probably because they never had a settlement as such. They lived in widely scattered farms with plenty of hot-blooded cattle around them. Perhaps that's the secret of their survival."

— o —

That afternoon the big helicopter shuttled back and forth between somewhere in Auckland City and Whenuapai. They sat at the window with the binoculars watching hour after hour, but learned little except that the military were still in the area.

The next day was Friday. Rick swam across Lucas Creek to a derelict boat-building yard, and came back with an aluminium dinghy which he pulled up into the trees. He spent half an hour stripping all the flotation material out of it. That evening, Mihi prepared a nice tea for the two of them. She had baked the grey duck she had caught with a snare on a long bamboo pole. With its stuffing of herbed sticky rice and edible fern, it made a tasty and satisfying meal.

That night the wind picked up and blew strongly until about midnight when it dropped and heavy rain started. It rained all through the Sabbath in an unceasing downpour. Over the evening meal Rick said, "In one of Spider's Bible classes he mentioned that Jesus upset the religious authorities because of the way that he himself observed the Sabbath. Is that correct?"

"Yes. The Gospels reveal that the Jewish leaders were angry with him because he broke the religious establishment's rules on Sabbath keeping."

"The rules of the religious establishment?"

"Yes. They weren't God's rules that he broke. The rules Jesus broke were the rules on Sabbath-keeping that had been made by men, such as their law preventing the splinting a person's broken a leg on the Sabbath. Jesus, on the other hand, healed sick people on the Sabbath, and was condemned by the religious authorities for doing so.

"Why would Jesus want to break their rules?" asked Rick.

"Well, just by fulfilling God's intention for the Sabbath, Jesus broke the Jewish rules on Sabbath keeping."

"So what is God's intention for the Sabbath?"

"The main purpose of the Sabbath is to provide a time each week when God and man can come together without any distractions, to build and maintain their relationship. On the Sabbath Jesus would go out of his way to minister to people through his gift of healing, in order to establish that relationship. But his actions created a conflict because the Jews forbade healing on the Sabbath. Jesus, however, would not allow anything to stop him bringing life to people on his holy day. But the Jews, in their determination to keep the Lord and needy people apart on the Sabbath, violated God's intention for the Sabbath."

"But didn't Jesus heal people on all days of the week?"

"Yes, he did. He never turned down anyone who came to him for help. But the Sabbath was the only day that he personally sought out people in order to heal them. And it was the only day on which he asked those he had healed to advertise what he had done for them. Jesus very deliberately broke man's rules on the Sabbath in order to reveal God's purpose for it."

"Wow! That's profound," responded Rick reflectively. "The Sabbath is the day that God intentionally comes to us so he can give us spiritual healing and eternal life."

"I like it too," said Mihi, snuggling up to Rick. "And don't forget that the Sabbath has not only been given to us to build a relationship with God; it has also been given to us to help build relationships with each other," she said.

"I'm sorry, sweetheart," apologised Rick. "Things have been hectic lately, and I've been so preoccupied with getting the *Wakamihi* ready, that the Sabbath has been mainly a sleep catchup time for me." Then with a gleam in his eye he added, "Wow! You are one heck of a woman. Come here."

"Riiicky!" cried Mihi in mock protest.

After sunset the rain eased a little and the wind began to pick up again.

Rick, who was standing, staring out the window, said, "Tonight would be a good night to up anchor and get out of here. If the military are around, this wet weather will have them demoralised, whereas this westerly wind is in our favour for a quick run down the harbour. Let's go out to the boat at eleven o'clock, cast off at midnight and depart using our night sail. What do you say?"

"All of a sudden I feel scared."

"Do I take that for a yes?"

Mihi nodded her head.

"Well, we should get some shut-eye because it's going to be a long night," said Rick, as he rolled himself into his blankets and fell instantly asleep.

Mihi, who was afraid they might oversleep, stayed awake. A few minutes before eleven she shook Rick awake. "Time to go," she said.

Rick sat up and rubbed his eyes. "I was having a scary dream about a bridge falling on us."

"A bridge? What bridge?"

"Dunno. Anyway," he said, glancing at his watch, "it's time for us to say "Haere ra" to good old Aotearoa."

At the *Wakamihi*, Rick screwed the drain plug out of the dinghy so that it filled with water and sank to the bottom. Inside the yacht, Mihi pulled the night sail out of the sail locker then stopped and asked, "What if the military visited the shed where you built this boat? We know they were over that way. They would have put two and two together and come up with an escape boat."

"Yes. I thought of that myself. We were so focused on getting the *Wakamihi* launched that we overlooked covering our tracks. Still, we don't know that they actually visited that building. And even if they did check it out, they still wouldn't have learnt anything about our plans."

After a while Mihi asked, "If you were the commander of the Australian troops, where would you station watchmen to keep an eye on boats moving in or out of the harbour?"

"Good question. At the narrowest points, I guess."

"And those would be…?"

"Where the two bridges cross the harbour."

"And if there were sentries on the bridges, what would they see?"

"Well, they might pick up our sail, but I doubt it, because they would be looking into the rain and wind and that would reduce their visibility somewhat."

"What if they had electronic sensors set under the bridges to pick up boats going past?"

"What if! What if!" Rick was becoming exasperated. "We'll never get out of here if we stop to consider every 'what if.'"

"Ricky, darling, I'm not trying to sabotage your vision. I just want us to succeed. There's far too much at stake for us to fail just because we overlooked something we should have considered."

"Well, what would you recommend?"

"Let's leave the driftwood on the front deck, and drop our sail once we get into the channel and allow the outgoing tide to carry us under the upper harbour bridge. That way, if we set off any alarms, we may only appear to be some derelict boat that the storm dislodged."

"I think you are unnecessarily over-cautious, but if it will give you peace of mind, I'll do what you suggest."

"Ricky, when your survival depends on being constantly alert and cautious, you develop a sixth sense about things. Besides, your dream could be a warning from the Lord."

"Do you really think so?"

"I do."

"Well, the tide doesn't flow with much force until after one in the morning. We could wait until then."

At quarter past one, Rick hoisted and tightened the sail, and once they had entered the channel that would carry them beneath the bridge, he dropped the sail onto the deck, anticipating a smooth ride through to the other side. Confident that everything would be okay, he remained in the small watertight compartment with the hatch open, in order to keep a better eye on things. By standing on his toes, he was able to look both fore and aft along the deck.

He was shocked, therefore, when a klaxon horn blasted the night air the moment the *Wakamihi* reached the centre of the bridge. An instant later there were shouts from the west bank, and two powerful searchlights on a pier on the southern side of the bridge began to sweep across the water towards the boat. Rick wished he could just shut the hatch and shout, "Dive! Dive! Dive!" But while most of the *Wakamihi* was below water, she was no submarine. In a few seconds the outgoing current carried her into the full glare of the sweeping beams. At first, both lights passed right over the boat. In the next sweep one paused momentarily, then moved on. But it soon returned and began to sweep the deck, and was joined by the other. There were more shouts and the sound of booted feet running down the pier. Guns were trained on the *Wakamihi* and bullets began ricocheting across the water.

"God, help us!" cried Rick.

At that moment two bursts of gunfire rang out from the eastern side of the bridge. One searchlight was extinguished and the second angled its beam up into the sky and stayed fixed in that position. "Is that you, J.B?" Rick wondered, looking over his shoulder. "It would be just like you to cover every possible exit to ensure that we got away safely."

Rick was in the process of hoisting the sail when a bullet went through it, stinging his eyes and face with bits of salty canvas. Staggering back with his hands over his eyes, he caught his left foot in the rudder rope and fell overboard. When the boat lurched to a new heading, Mihi popped her head out to see what had happened. When she couldn't see Rick, she hoisted herself out onto the deck and immediately noticed his leg tangled in the rope. Throwing herself down beside him, she reached for his belt and with all her strength she hauled him high enough so that he could grab the tiller rope and help pull himself back on board.

Back on deck, Rick lay retching and spewing up seawater, all the while signalling frantically to Mihi with one hand to get the boat back on course and the sail fully up. More bullets and two rocket-propelled grenades were fired into the night, but the shooting was hasty and wild, and they sailed beyond it.

Down below, Rick massaged his sore stomach and changed into dry clothes. "Thanks sweetheart," he groaned. "That was close. The immediate danger is over." He then gave her an account of what had happened topside.

"Those shots from the eastern side would be J.B.'s doing," she said confidently.

"Can we be sure someone will be covering the main harbour crossing too?"

"Knowing J.B., I'm confident he'll have it sorted. You can be sure of that."

"Now that we have been detected, the military will be waiting for us there. Nothing's more certain."

"What's the alternative?"

"We could hide in the mangroves at Henderson Creek."

"Will we be safe there?"

"No. We'd be trapped. They will search every waterway by day until they find us. And the guard on the main harbour bridge would be alerted and doubled. My instinct is to make a run for it before they can do bring the rest of their troops together to focus their entire efforts on us. What do you say?"

"I'm with you. We're blessed to have such a strong wind on our starboard quarter. At least we are not being slowed by tacking."

"Best to keep the boat on its present course."

As the main harbour bridge loomed closer, Rick could feel his heart beginning to race. Through the driving rain he could see flashes of light up on the bridge; some flashes were brighter than others, but they were a mystery to him. As the *Wakamihi* sailed past the old Chelsea Sugar Works, he detected a flickering light at sea level to the left of the harbour bridge. His Morse Code was very rusty, but he was able to read: *da-da, dit-dit, dit-dit-dit-dit, dit-dit*. Then the message repeated: *da-da, dit-dit, dit-dit-dit-dit, dit-dit*. Well, that wasn't difficult. It spelled Mihi. Only someone from Waitak would know that Mihi was on board. Remaining ever ready to take evasive action if necessary, Rick took a risk and guided the boat towards the signals coming from the circular building at the base of the northern end of the bridge.

Rick's anxiety was relieved when a lone figure came running down the pier and shone torchlight on his own face. It was Flip, the Taranaki lad. As Rick came alongside and dropped the sail, Flip called out, "All the channels between the bridge piers have cables across them. There's a possibility that the main channels are mined. We've cut through the cable in this channel," he said, indicating which one with his outstretched arm. "You will be safe if you sail through on the left of this first pier."

"What were those flashes of light I saw up on the bridge?"

"We had a bit of a gun battle with the Aussies."

"Anyone get hurt?"

"Uh-huh. Two of our folk got killed. The Aussies used rocket-propelled grenades.

"Who got killed?"

"You don't want to know."

"Tell me!" cried Rick.

"J.B. and Carla."

"Noooo! Noooo!" wailed Rick. "Not them."

"Look! We've sunk one of their boats and cleared away the guards from the deck of the bridge. But you have to get moving before they regroup." As he spoke, bullets came ricocheting across the water in their direction.

"Here," Flip said, picking up a large bundle. "This is for Mihi from the ladies. Best of luck, matey. We're all relying on you. Now get the hell out of here!"

With hot tears flooding his eyes, Rick squeezed the bundle down the front hatch to Mihi and then hoisted the sail. With the bridge receding behind them, and just when he thought they were beyond trouble, Rick heard an outboard motor coming diagonally towards them from the city side of the harbour. As it got closer to their boat, he was able to pick out a three-metre dinghy with two armed soldiers and an outboard operator. When they signalled to him to heave-to, he let the sail go slack and raised his hands, telling Mihi at the same time to stay below, out of sight. As they attempted to come alongside, he noticed, to his satisfaction, that they were not experienced boatmen.

"Your journey's over, mate," smirked one of the soldiers. "We're taking you back with us."

They were apparently unaware of Mihi's presence on the boat. "Keep your hands up where we can see them and step carefully into our dinghy," ordered a soldier.

But, instead of stepping into the dinghy, Rick stood on its nearest gunwale, easing his weight down gradually and unbalancing their craft. "Bloody hell!" shouted one of the Aussies as the three of them moved to the opposite side to counter Rick's weight. Quickly, Rick stepped back onto the *Wakamihi*. As the side of the dinghy nearest him popped up, he put his foot against it, thrusting it upwards and outwards with all his might, capsizing the dingy on top of its occupants.

With a racing heart, Rick turned and tightened *Wakamihi*'s night sail. Soon they were sailing down the harbour past Devonport and North Head. Once out into the channel, he felt safer. But just as they began to relax, their ears caught the sound of a high-revving motor and their pulse-rates increased as a motor boat came racing towards them. Rick dropped the sail and lay flat on the deck, hoping that the stinging rain in the eyes of those on the speeding motor-boat would make the *Wakamihi* invisible. The motor boat sped past, then angled back a further hundred metres out. Each time the boat returned, it was further and further away.

Down below, Mihi opened the rain-dampened parcel. Inside she found Rick's shield with the boar's tusks mounted on it, two loaves of freshly baked pumpkin bread, a cheese and some home-made butter all wrapped up in the hand-made quilt that had been given them as a wedding present. There was a letter with it, signed by the women of the ladies' group.

When Rick came down below and saw that Mihi had been crying again, he gave her a hug. She handed him the letter. Holding the steering wheel with one hand, and the letter in the other, he read:

"Dear Mihi,

While this letter is mainly for you, we're also writing it for Rick. We heard, from J.B., how you saved the lives of others by shooting the Australian soldier. We know you well enough to realise how terribly upset you will be over that. Unfortunately, life in this world does not always present us with choices between good and evil. More often, the choices are between a greater and a lesser evil. But you, like the true Christian you are, made the correct choice—though it was a very painful one—and, as a result you have undoubtedly saved many lives. We know you well enough to realise that you acted out of love for others, not out of hatred for the deceased soldier. We wish that we could gather around you and give you a big hug. Every one of us is praying that God will ease the pain that you will be experiencing. And we know he will."

The letter went on to say:

"We are all very traumatised at having lost Cardiac and our homes at Waitak. Actually, we are so mixed up by recent events we're finding it difficult to think rationally. We have decided to bury Cardiac in the square of the settlement that he had been chairman of for the last six years. Unfortunately, many of our personal treasures have been destroyed along with our homes. Our hopes for the future, and especially for the next generation, are now in the Lord's care, and with you both. We are praying that he will take you and Rick safely across the sea to your destination. We want you to know that we love you both very, very much, and that, in addition to our regular times of prayer, someone will be praying for you around the clock every day until you return. We have divided each week into one hundred and sixty-eight one-hour segments, and every hour will be covered by someone praying for your safety and success."

The letter concluded with an excerpt from Psalm 107:

"Others went out on the sea in ships . . . they cried out to the Lord in their trouble, and he brought them out of their distress. He stilled the storm to a

whisper; the waves of the sea were hushed. They were glad when it grew calm, and he guided them to their desired haven. Let them give thanks to the Lord."

When Rick had finished reading the letter, Mihi asked him what the man on the pier had said. But it was too soon to tell her about J.B. and Carla. Rick was having enough difficulty keeping his own emotions under control, and it was important that he keep a perfectly level head if their mission was to succeed. He could not allow the fact that the Australian military had killed four settlement people in four days to distract him, so he just said to Mihi, "J.B. discovered that there were cables across all the channels under the bridge. They thought they may have been mined. There was a bit of a gun battle to drive the troops off the northern side of the bridge so they could cut the cable there. They sent me a message in Morse code to get me to sail through the channel they had cleared. Thanks to them we are now clear of the inner harbour."

"Were any of our folk hurt in the battle?"

"Grab the wheel," grimaced Rick as he rushed to the toilet and retched several times.

When he came out Mihi asked, "Are you okay, Ricky?"

"I think it's just the tension," he replied. "I'll be fine."

"Where to from here?"

"It will soon be morning and the patrol aircraft will be out. It's my guess that they will already be airborne. What they won't know is the direction we'll be taking. I expect they'll assume we will sail north, so we'll do the opposite and go south. But in order to sail south we have to get around the Coromandel Peninsula."

Rick pulled out a chart of the Gulf and, tapping a spot with a finger, he said, "There's no way we can get around the Peninsula before daybreak, so we'll sail south and hide out on the mainland coast opposite Waiheke Island."

"Here," he pointed. "This would be the least likely place they would expect us to go. We'll hide out there for a couple of days while they search the anchorages of the outer islands for us. Once we think they've had enough time to do that we'll set sail for the Mercury Islands. After a week the pressure should be off. We'll then sail southeast to catch the trade winds to Chile."

It was an hour after daybreak before Rick found a suitable spot and anchored the *Wakamihi* in a small creek. To the north they could hear maritime patrol aircraft sweeping back and forth, but none came their way.

Rick couldn't bring himself to tell Mihi about Carla and J.B., but on Monday afternoon she brought up the subject of the battle on the harbour bridge again. When Rick told her that Carla and J.B. had been killed in the fight to secure a channel for the *Wakamihi* to pass through, Mihi was stunned. Sitting on the edge of her bunk with her head in her hands, she rocked back and forth wailing. "Oh God, how long, how long?" she cried, over and over.

Rick knelt in front of her and wrapped his arms around her waist. Their tears flowed together. Twice that night Rick was awakened by Mihi's sobbing. He found he could no longer make excuses in his own thinking for the behaviour of politicians and military leaders who were so inhumane in their treatment of people whom they wrongly considered were a threat to them.

CHAPTER ELEVEN

At about seven on Tuesday evening, Rick and Mihi hauled up their anchor and set sail for the Mercury Islands. For the first five hours it was brisk sailing, but then the wind dropped. By midnight the sky cleared and they were totally becalmed. Just before sunrise, a blanket of sea fog rolled over them, and they thanked God for it. Even though it was more comfortable down below than on top, they were glad to get out the cabin where they had been confined for the past few days. To break the monotony and to get his mind relaxed, Rick decided to do a spot of fishing. He'd hardly dropped his line over the side when he heard men's voices. They weren't talking very loudly but their words came clearly across the flat water.

"Wait! Wait! Wait!" complained one impatiently. "All we seem to do is wait! Quite frankly, I'm fed up with waiting! It's my bet that they're half way to the Cooks."

"Not according to Corporal Reed," replied the other. "He reckons they're too smart to do the obvious."

"There's talk going round that Reed was thrown into the brig for reasons other than the failure of his men to contain the Kiwis on Herald Island."

"Yeah! Reed has been mouthing off to everyone that the Kiwis are not diseased animals waiting to infect the rest of the world with their deadly virus. He claims that they are a very healthy, well-organised and intelligent alliance. 'A lot more civilised than we are,' were his exact words. He reckoned that we had no right to be killing innocent people. The chiefs weren't very pleased to hear that and decided to shut him down. But they'd left it a bit late."

"I'm inclined to agree with Reed. Every time we think we've got these Kiwis cornered, they slip out of our hands and leave us looking like a bunch of dingoes."

"You know what I think? I think the so-called Leoenzide epidemic is just a cover that our politicians are using as an excuse to get rid of the Kiwis. They know that as long as any Kiwis stay alive in New Zealand, the country belongs to them. But if they can get rid of all the Kiwis, then they can colonise the country and make it an Aussie state. The Indonesians had a go, but failed. Now we Aussies are having our turn. That's what I reckon. Except that we aren't doing any better than the Indos."

Just then a fish took the bait on Rick's line. It was a big one, possibly a kingfish, and it caught him by surprise and off balance. The yank on his line almost pulled him into the water. Falling sideways rather heavily, Rick rolled onto his right elbow to stop himself sliding off into the sea.

"What the heck was that?" one of the men asked.

"Yeah. Not the sort of thing you'd expect to hear out here."

Rick lay where he fell, not daring to move, and Mihi froze. The silence was intense. Billows of fog swept by, and very briefly, through a gap in the mist, Mihi glimpsed the silhouette of a submarine on the surface.

"Hey, Mace! Over there! Look! It's a boat, low in the water. There's a couple of people on it."

"Where? I don't see anything," replied Mace, who had clearly seen both the yacht and Mihi.

"It was just there. I saw it through a gap in the fog."

"You know what I think," said Mace with a change of voice. "I think we've talked ourselves into seeing what's not really there. We've been up here too long."

"No! I really did see it."

"Chauncy, believe me, you didn't see it! The consequences of seeing a boat out here with people in it are not ones that you could live with. You're a good man, Chauncy. Let your conscience guide you for once. I assure you, you will enjoy your sleep much better if you choose not to report what you 'imagined,' rather than carrying the burden, for the rest of your life, of causing the deaths of innocent people."

The long silence that followed was interrupted by an officer climbing down from the conning tower onto the fore deck to join the two men.

Chauncy spoke first. "You know what I think, sir? If people have escaped from this land, it's my bet they're halfway to the Cooks."

"I'm inclined to agree with you, there, sailor," replied the officer. "In fact, I came to the conclusion an hour ago that we were wasting our time sitting around here, so I called base and we have been given permission to move off at 0930 hours. Both of you go below now and report to Chief Petty Officer Cousins."

Rick and Mihi didn't speak to each other until the submarine motored away on the surface.

"Whew!" uttered Rick. "My heart was thumping so loudly I was scared they would hear it."

"After what we heard from those men," said Mihi reflectively, "do you think we need to have a stopover at the Mercury Islands?"

"A stopover will definitely improve our chances," said Rick. "Let them search the oceans for us, and then, when they have given up, we'll move off. I also need an opportunity to check the boat before we commit ourselves to a major ocean voyage. Even though this leg of the journey hasn't been a real test for her, I'd like to know how she has handled it before we lose sight of land. Anyway, I'm keen to see what this fish tastes like. How about putting it on the pan and frying it in some of that home-made butter?"

At the Mercury Islands, it was six hours before Rick found a suitably smooth beach in a narrow cover where he could run the *Wakamihi* up at high tide. Large pohutukawa trees grew out over the sand and would provide good shelter. But he would need to wait until low tide to ensure he could get the boat on and off the beach without damaging the hull.

The next day, they ran the boat ashore. Mihi carried the anchor up the beach and dug it in among the pohutukawa roots. Rick then tied the anchor rope to the hardwood bollard on the deck to hold the boat firmly on the beach while the tide retreated. As the tide went out, Rick positioned manuka props beneath the bilge keels of the *Wakamihi*, to keep the boat upright. Where the sand was soft, he dug down deep and placed rocks into the bottom of the hole before tamping the prop into place on top of it.

He was genuinely pleased that such an old boat, which had been out of the water for over four decades, had done so well. On Sunday, Rick did a bit of caulking that was required in a couple of places, and hammered in some copper nails where they were needed. Over all, the boat was in pretty good shape and he was pleased with it. He decided to put it back in the water the very next high tide.

While Rick worked on the yacht, Mihi constructed a shelter beneath a large totara tree on the grassy flat just beyond the beach. In an effort to conserve the boat's rations, she introduced Rick to *kaimoana*—seafood, Aotearoa style. For the next seven days, they had meals of mussels (Rick's favourite) with puha and some salty edible sea weed, paua and shore celery, and snapper with steamed edible fern. Apart from one brief shower, the weather was sunny and pleasant, enabling them to relax and catch up on missed sleep.

At midday on Thursday, Rick filled the boat's water tank from a nearby creek and, after they had committed themselves and their boat to the Lord, they set off for the journey down through the South Pacific. Once they turned around East Cape and set their course for the Southern Ocean, the breeze picked up and they had several days of brisk sailing. On the fifth day, they ran into a heavy swell and a strong south-westerly wind. Mihi, who wasn't feeling very well, stayed in her bunk all day. Just after dark, there was an awful crash. The boat shuddered under the impact of something very heavy. There was a splintering of wood, and a jet of water sprayed into the bunkroom above Mihi's head. She screamed, rolled out of her bunk onto her hands and feet and scuttled out of the way. The jolt of the collision was followed by a shuddering, graunching sound as a weighty object scraped down the side of the boat and then disappeared aft.

"Start pumping!" yelled Rick as he grabbed the hand-made quilt and tried to ram it into the triangular-shaped hole in the hull. The force of the water, however, was so great that his best efforts only resulted in fanning the jet of water around the cabin. Both he and the bunk were quickly saturated and the bilge began to overflow above the flooring. "Mihi! I need something to help ram this quilt into the hole! Quick! Anything like a broom handle will do."

Mihi grabbed the automatic out of its clips on the bulkhead and passed it to him. Using the barrel as a ramrod, he forced the quilt through the hole until there was a bulk of material outside the hull like a cork. With further ramming he was able to reduce the flow until only a trickle of water continued to run down the inside from the saturated bed cover.

"Whatever was that?" called Mihi from the hand-pump.

"Probably a container that washed off some ship during a storm. They float around for years in ocean currents, just below the surface, and are a real danger to shipping."

"What are we going to do now?"

"Well, we are lucky it wasn't any worse. At least we've got the leak contained for the moment. If we run into a big storm, however, we'll be in serious trouble. I suspect that the hull has been significantly weakened in a line aft of the puncture. Anyway, the first thing we need to do is get the bilge pumped out."

"Then what?"

"We'll need to get to the nearest land to assess the damages and fix the boat."

Both Rick and Mihi sweated at the pumps for over half an hour before they'd emptied the bilge. Rick then checked his GPS and looked at his maps.

"Our best bet will be the Chatham Islands," he said. "If the present conditions continue, we should be able to make landfall by Friday morning."

Mihi's sleeping bag was sodden so Rick suggested that she use his bunk while he sailed the boat through the night. If she was feeling better by morning, she could do a couple of hours on the wheel while he had a snooze.

After Mihi had cleaned up the cabin and hung her sleeping bag out to dry, she got out her Bible and spent several minutes looking through the Psalms. Eventually she exclaimed, "Hah! Found it!" She stood up and came to Rick. "Listen to this," she said. "The seas have lifted up, O Lord, the seas have lifted up their voice; the seas have lifted up their pounding waves. Mightier than the thunder of the great waters, mightier than the breakers of the sea—

the Lord on high is mighty." She looked at Rick's face for a response.

"Where is that written?" he asked.

"In Psalm 93. Did you notice that it says God is mightier than the sea?"

"Yes. I needed to be reminded of that. We have to trust Him."

By morning of the second day the wind eased, though the swell was still running high. It was with some relief that they sailed into the lee of the first of the Chatham Islands a few hours later. Rick decided to take the boat to the main island where there would be a wharf, and, hopefully, a ship-servicing yard of some sort where he could make the necessary repairs. As far as he could remember, the inhabitants of the Chathams—who were unaffected by the plague—were taken to Australia because they were no longer able to get either service or supplies from New Zealand, or to sell their produce there. The location was just too remote to be viable.

Once the boat was tied up at the wharf, Rick put on goggles and went over the side to check the damage. Mihi sat on the wharf waiting for him. When he came up, he looked very serious and discouraged. "How bad is it?" Mihi asked in a quiet voice.

Rick massaged his forehead with his left hand. "It's a lot worse than I expected. We were lucky to get here. In a couple of places, the container, or whatever it was, peeled away large portions of the outer layer of timber. It's a shredded mess. If I had the gear, I could clean it back and fill and patch it with fibre-glass, but that would take the best part of a week."

"It looks like there are some boat construction or servicing yards back there," said Mihi, indicating with her hand. "Why don't you go and do a search for the materials you need while I set up home in one of those houses. I'll find a dry and cosy one with a good water tank, give the place a quick clean, and then shift up to it whatever we'll need over the next few days. I'll make a nice dinner for us, and we can rest for the next twenty-four hours to get our strength and enthusiasm back."

Rick went on a search for the materials he needed to repair the hull, but found nothing suitable.

With not enough spring lines to allow *Wakamihi* to move freely up and down with the tide at the wharf, Rick sailed the boat to a buoy up the bay and secured it there. He then went over the side with a tin of grease he had found in a shed and worked it into the cloth that protruded from the hole, waterproofing it as much as possible. That way he could sleep soundly without worrying about the boat filling with water overnight. When he had finished, he waved to Mihi, who rowed out to get him in a dinghy they had found.

The sun set that Friday evening about an hour later than it did in Auckland, for which Mihi was glad. It gave her the extra time she needed to get the house ready. She even had time to collect several armfuls of driftwood from the beach and light a fire in the grate to help dry out the house and make it a little cosier. The dancing green and blue flames gave them a focal point for the evening and helped take Rick's mind off the fact that he had not been able to find any fibreglass resins that hadn't 'gone off' years ago.

Rick spread out his wet shorts and shirt to dry, then they sat down and read some Psalms and sang a few Waitak praise songs together, but without much enthusiasm. Rick's favourite song, 'Ziklag's Ashes', however, brightened him up and breathed some hope into their current situation. Mihi said wistfully, "Someone back home will be praying for us at this very instant." After a pause she added, "And someone would have been praying for us at the moment of that collision. We have to believe that God's hand is over everything that happens to us. I have confidence that it will eventually work out according to his plan."

"Would you say that it was God's will for Ari, Cardiac, J.B. and Carla to die?" asked Rick quietly.

"Dad calls it God's permissive will," she replied. "In other words, while God didn't plan it that way, he allowed it to happen. And after the resurrection, those four people will be honoured as martyrs. They gave their lives that others might live. That's a great honour that will be theirs throughout all eternity. If we look at events purely from the perspective of this life, they often don't make sense."

"Well, I suppose that if we looked at the collision of the *Wakamihi* and the container through God's eyes too, then we should look for the positive rather than the negative outcome."

"Now that's more like it," affirmed Mihi with a smile.

After a while she asked, "Have you thought about how we will get away from the Chathams, and what our destination will be now that the *Wakamihi* is in such bad shape?

"Yes. I was hoping I'd find another boat here. It seems, however, that the Chatham Islanders took their ocean-going boats with them when they left."

After a minute of thoughtful silence Mihi said, "My Dad had a ditty that went something like this:

> *"High aspirations you may have,*
> *And many noble dreams,*
> *But you must build your road to the mountain,*
> *And your bridges to its streams."*

"Meaning? In our case?"

"For us it means that we may have to give up our dream of getting to South America in favour of something more realistic in the present circumstances."

"Well, I feel certain that God has not brought us this far to abandon us now."

"Me too."

They prayed together and felt much better.

Early next morning they awoke to a brightly coloured sky.

"Red sky in the morning, sailor's warning," muttered Rick.

"Well, it's not raining yet, so let's go for a walk before our morning meal," suggested Mihi.

They hadn't been walking along the wide beach more than thirty minutes when it started to drizzle, so they returned to the house. The rain set in and it rained all day, the skies clearing just on sunset. They were glad of the opportunity to rest, and after reading the Bible and praying together once again, they spent most of the time catching up on lost sleep.

CHAPTER TWELVE

While Mihi was preparing food for breakfast next morning she glanced out the window and called excitedly, "There's a boat coming into the harbour."

Rick pulled his binoculars from their case and ran to the window. A very rusty steel ship, about twenty metres long, was coming around the point. It had a faded number and a Japanese name on its bow. "It looks like a whale catcher," commented Rick.

"It can't be," said Mihi. "This area is part of the Southern Ocean Whale Sanctuary."

"Well, that's definitely a harpoon gun mounted in the bows," he announced.

"Why don't I have a good feeling about this boat?" Mihi asked herself out aloud.

The ship remained out in the bay until high tide, then moved up beside the wharf until it came aground in the shallows. Three crew members secured it to the bollards on the wharf and fastened cables to the base of the crane on the stern deck. A few minutes later a party of five Japanese seamen came ashore and entered the marine workshops, walking right past the house, which allowed Rick and Mihi were able to get a good look at them. About half an hour later, they came back along the road carrying an assortment of tools and other equipment.

"I'm going to have a talk with them," Rick said.

"Be careful, Ricky," said Mihi.

"Let me take your gun," he replied.

Rick slipped out the back door, ran down the rear of the next house, and stepped out onto the road in front of the returning seamen. As soon as they saw him, their eyes and mouths dropped open. A bucket-load of gear slipped from the hand of one man onto the road with a crash. It was obvious they were not expecting to find anyone on the island. Rick took the initiative. "What are you doing?" he demanded sternly.

"Ah please," replied the spokesman, "ship's hull is damage. Ice. And heat-exchanger not work properly. We fix."

"Who is your captain?"

"Please, captain on boat."

"What is your captain's name?"

"Name?"

"Yes, Captain's name."

"Ah, Captain Mori."

"I want to talk to Captain Mori."

"You want talk to Captain Mori?"

"Yes."

"Okay. You come," he said, leading the way.

The captain, seeing Rick coming down the wharf with his men, came out and stood at the rail. There was a sharp exchange between him and the spokesman of the group in high-pressure Japanese.

Rick waited patiently until he was finished and then said to the captain, "Sir, I would like to talk to you."

"Who are you?" the captain asked in tolerably good English.

"I am Rick Carter, from Port Douglas in Queensland, Australia."

"What are you doing here in Chatham Islands?"

"He's got a cheek asking me what I am doing here," thought Rick. "What is *he* doing here?" But he kept a straight face and replied, "My yacht got blown down to New Zealand in a storm. I'm trying to get back to Australia with my wife."

"Your wife? Where's your wife?" the captain asked bluntly, looking over Rick's shoulder.

"In a house back there," indicated Rick with a sweep of his hand.

"Where is your boat?" the captain asked.

"I'm afraid it was damaged beyond repair," said Rick. "We're lucky to have survived." He hoped that no one on the Japanese vessel would look too closely at the *Wakamihi* tied to the buoy up the bay.

"I cannot take you," the captain said rather tersely. "We have no room for passengers. Besides, we've still got three weeks of work before we return to Japan."

"I can pay you," Rick said.

The captain laughed. "I have no use for Australian money."

"I will pay you in gold ingots."

The captain looked at Rick with a quizzical look on his face. "Gold?" he asked.

"Yes. Gold."

"You are joking, surely."

"No, I am not joking. I will pay you in gold to take my wife and me to Japan with you. I am a sailor and I can help you on your boat, if necessary."

"I would like to see your gold first," he said with disbelieving smile.

"I will bring it to you, tomorrow morning. And if you are willing to help us, we shall draw up a contract," said Rick.

"Do not bring gold to this ship. I will meet you at that end of the wharf at 0700 hours tomorrow," he said, pointing to where the wharf abutted the land.

"That's fine with me. Good day to you, sir."

Rick returned to the house by a roundabout route so that no one watching from the Japanese boat would be able to determine exactly where he and Mihi were staying.

When the tide went out, Rick and Mihi observed the Japanese examining the hull of the ship on the side away from the wharf. Later they could see flashes from an arc welder and hear the banging of big hammers on steel plate.

That night, after dark, Rick paddled cautiously out to the *Wakamihi* and removed from the yacht everything they might need. He sealed the boat up and hooked some giant kelp around the base of the mast to make it appear as though it had been there a long time. Back at the house, he and Mihi sat in the dark and worked out their strategy for the next day.

At seven sharp the next morning, both Rick and Captain Mori arrived at the chosen rendezvous. Rick passed a gold ingot to the captain who bounced it up and down in the palm of his hand, checking its weight, before turning it over and studying the imprint of the dove and the cross. He then bit it and examined the marks left by his teeth.

"Good," he smiled. "Very good. I want three thousand U.S. dollars in gold for you, and three thousand for your wife."

"That's too much," replied Rick. "I'll pay you one thousand dollars each. And we want a cabin to ourselves."

They haggled back and forth and finally settled on a total of four thousand U.S. dollars in gold ingots for a cabin back to Japan. They would get one meal of rice a day. They were also required to remain in their cabin at all times, except for thirty minutes after dark each night. Rick said he would make duplicate copies of the agreement which they would sign and date, and he assured the captain that he would hand over the gold as soon as they were settled in their cabin.

By Wednesday the Japanese whale-catcher was ready to sail, and Rick and Mihi turned up at the wharf with their gear. As they came aboard, the seamen glanced sideways at Mihi and talked among themselves. Rick guessed that they were commenting on her racial origin.

The cabin appeared to have been a rope locker. One wall was lined with deep shelving. All the inside walls were cold, painted steel, but the deck beneath was warm, being above the engine room. There were two chairs and a small table in the cabin, which looked as though they had been taken from a home on the island. The table had been fastened to one wall, possibly to prevent it falling over in rough weather. There was also a covered bucket in the corner, which Rick presumed was to be their toilet.

Rick and Mihi placed their mattresses and sleeping bags on the floor and stashed the rest of their gear in the deep shelves.

They didn't have long to wait until the captain showed up. He came in and shut the door behind him. Rick produced a small soft leather bag with the correct amount of gold in it. The captain opened the bag and poured the contents onto the table. He examined each ingot, as he did the one that Rick had shown him on Sunday, before replacing them in the bag and hooking it to a spring scale that he pulled from his pocket. He then scribbled some figures in a notebook, drew a line beneath them and worked out the answer. Snapping the notebook shut he smiled, "Good! Very good!"

They both signed and dated the agreements, each keeping a copy. "You will be in Japan in about one month. By the way, do you have passports?"

"I'm afraid all our documents were lost with the boat."

"Do you realise that if I take you to Japan, I'll have to hand you over to Customs?"

"Yes. That's understood. My embassy will care for us once we get there."

"The cook will bring you a bowl of boiled rice once a day."

"Thank you," said Rick. "Do you have a key for the door?"

"There is no key for this door. But you will be quite safe," he smiled. "There is nowhere for a bad person to escape to."

After the captain had gone Rick levered a four-by-two off the front of the shelving. He then angled it across the inside of the door, through the handle, so the door could not be opened from the outside.

"I feel a bit more secure, and will sleep better knowing that no one can just walk in at will," Rick muttered.

There was one porthole to the cabin, but the view of the ocean was partly obscured by a small derrick on the side of the ship.

Once outside the harbour, the chaser would pitch, roll and yawn in the heavy seas, so Rick suggested to Mihi that she would be much more comfortable if she lay down on her mattress on the floor, which would be as near as possible to the fulcrum of the ship's movement—the most comfortable place in their 'cabin.'

"While you are lying there," he said to Mihi, "devise some sort of exercise programme to help keep us fit, and some way to stimulate our minds and spirits. This cabin will be our prison for a month and we need something to relieve the boredom and keep our bodies, minds and spirits active."

The first day they talked about the interesting places they had each been to. On the second they shared their most embarrassing moments. And so it went. Meal times were always a welcome break. The cook, Akira, who brought them their boiled rice, occasionally smuggled in some fish as well which was greatly appreciated, and Rick determined to reward the man well for his kindness. One day when the cook came in, he noticed a Bible on the table. Pointing to it he asked, "Bible?"

"Yes," replied Mihi, "It's a Bible."

"You Christian?" he asked in heavily accented English.

"Yes, we're Christians," responded Mihi.

"Me Christian too. Not good Christian. But Jesus is number one Boss." After that they often had a short prayer with Akira, which he seemed to appreciate. They also welcomed him with a warm hug each day and gave him small presents of dehydrated fruits from their meagre supply.

On the second night, Rick was wakened by someone trying to get into their cabin. He went to the door and called out, "Who's there? What do you want?" All he heard was the sound of retreating footsteps.

The attempted intrusion never happened again. Several times each day Rick checked their position on his GPS against the map of the Southern Ocean he had retrieved from the *Wakamihi*. South of

Campbell Island, their boat joined a larger fleet of whalers. They heard the explosion of the harpoon gun and the victorious shouts of the sailors. Their boat then towed the whale carcass to the mother ship and there was a loud exchange of friendly banter between the two crews.

Ten days later, on Sunday, when Akira brought them their steamed rice at ten in the morning, he looked rather sombre. Mihi, who was very perceptive, asked, "What's wrong, Akira? You look sad."

"Yes, Missus," Akira replied, "I really sad. Not good for you."

Suddenly aware that Akira was taking about them, Rick asked, "What's not good for us, Akira?"

"I hear captain talk on radio. He not know I hear him. He say, 'I want reward for New Zealand people.'"

"Yes. What else did you hear?"

"I not hear anymore because crewman come. Captain just say, 'Yes, yes. Tomorrow, 1900 hours.'"

When Akira had gone Mihi said, "You should give him a gold ingot. He's risked himself for us."

"I will," said Rick. "But it wouldn't be wise to give it to him yet. If it were discovered, it could get him and us into a lot of trouble. We have to decide what we are going to do. It's my guess that we are to be handed over to some Australian vessel tomorrow. And you can bet your bottom dollar that we will be put over the side without our guns or gold. We need to pray about this. A big storm before pickup time would be very welcome."

"What Australian vessel would be in this area?"

"I have no idea. Possibly a patrol craft or another fishing vessel. I don't know."

"What is our position at the moment?" Mihi asked.

"We're between Macquarie Island and the Auckland Islands."

"Which are we nearer to?"

"The Auckland Islands."

"Let's go there."

"You mean, take over this ship?" questioned Rick incredulously.

"Yes."

"Piracy is a capital offence."

"Ricky, if we hijack this ship, no one will die. But if we don't, there is a strong possibility that not only will we die, but all our folk back in Aotearoa also. You know that, don't you? Besides, this fleet is engaged in illegal whaling, so why would they want to take us back to civilisation where we could expose them? And from what Akira has told us, the evidence strongly suggests that the captain has no intention of keeping his side of the contract we made with him. I have no sympathy for him."

"You never cease to surprise me," snickered Rick. "You're such a tender-hearted beautiful woman, yet you have the determination of a high-flying executive out for a major kill." "Whatever. But we need to act soon."

They spent half an hour considering their options. Rick and Mihi then put on their backpacks, containing the rest of the gold plus what remained of their food and clothing, and made their way to the bridge, conscious of the stares of the seamen. When they opened the bridge door, a blast of cold air swept in. The captain turned and upon seeing Rick and Mihi his face went red with anger. He was about to shout something when Rick pointed his automatic at his midriff. Stepping back in surprise and whispered hoarsely, "What you want?"

"We want to go to Enderby Island in the Auckland Islands," said Rick.

"I will need to get permission to leave the fleet," the captain said, reaching for the radio microphone.

"No radio!" commanded Mihi.

"Just a short call," he said, flicking a switch.

Mihi raised her pistol and fired a bullet into the radio. Both the captain and the seaman on the wheel jumped away from the shower of sparks that cascaded down.

"I said no radio!"

"You wrecked my radio!" the captain blurted.

"Serves you right!" said Rick forcefully. "You were up to no good. If you needed permission from the mother ship you would have used the small radio, not that one. Do you take us for fools? Now please get this ship pointed towards the Auckland Islands. If you get us there safely, we will spare your life. If you try to trick us, we will shoot you."

Captain Mori checked his chart and sullenly commanded the seaman on the wheel to steer the ship onto a new bearing.

Both Rick and Mihi knew that leaving the ship would be the most dangerous part for them, so they decided to take the captain with them until they were safely on land. At ten in the morning, when the cook came with food for the bridge crew, Rick acted very casually, as though everything was okay, and asked him to bring their food to the bridge also. After they had finished eating, Rick collected the dishes. When the cook returned, Rick turned his back to the others and, with the cook watching, pushed a gold ingot beneath the plates as he handed them to him. With an expressionless face, the cook bowed and departed.

At first light next morning, a call came through from the factory ship. The captain said it was a regular scheduled call and he would be expected to report his position. Rick stepped up to the radio and turned it off, telling the captain in no uncertain terms that if he went anywhere near this radio, he would destroy it also. An hour later, the grey hills of the Auckland Islands appeared through the rain. Rick directed the captain to sail his ship into Port Ross and put them ashore at Sandy Bay on the south west of Enderby Island. The captain brought his ship to a semi-circular bay and shouted commands to the crew, who let the anchor go with a roar of rattling chain. The weather was sleety, cold and uninviting, but that was the least of Rick's and Mihi's worries as a dinghy was lowered over the side.

"Captain," said Rick. "No one else is to leave this ship. Just you, my wife and me."

"I'm not leaving!" he said through clenched teeth.

"Oh yes, you are!" replied Rick firmly, indicating with a swing of his automatic's barrel that the captain should go over the side into the dinghy. "Once we get safely to shore, you may return with the dinghy." Mihi went over the side first, followed by their hostage, and then Rick with their gear. Rick started the outboard motor and guided the dinghy onto the beach between a couple of huge bull sealions that did nothing more than roll their heads over their shoulders to peer in their direction. Mihi stepped out holding her gun, followed by Rick with their gear.

"You are free to return to your ship now," said Rick. "The gold I gave you to take us to Japan will more than cover the cost of a new radio and the extra hours of sailing we required of you." The captain curled his lip and spat with a forward thrust of his head. Rick put his foot against the dinghy's transom and shoved it back out into the cold sea with such a jerk the captain had to grasp the gunwales with both hands to stop falling backwards into the water. Sitting stiffly upright with a sour look on his face, Captain Mori started the outboard and returned to his ship.

"I wish I felt confident that that's the last we'll see of him," said Mihi. Then she added, "I'm freezing!"

"There will be a building here somewhere," Rick responded. Every year a group of ornithologists come here to study the Gibson's Albatrosses that nest on this island. There might even be a food store if we are lucky. We need to find it before we get hypothermia. It's my guess that it won't be too far away."

By the time they found the building and got themselves inside, Rick's fingers were white to the second joint. Inside, he almost cried with agony as his hands thawed in his armpits.

"How did you know about the resident albatrosses?" Mihi asked.

"I've been a keen bird watcher ever since I was a young kid. I subscribe to several Australian ornithological magazines and journals. Anyway, we are out of luck. There is no food here," said Rick, as he closed the last cupboard. "I guess they'd bring what they need with them as there's too much of a risk of stashed food being stolen by crews of visiting fishing boats."

Later in the afternoon when Rick went to check the bay, the whale chaser was still anchored there.

"I don't like that one bit," he said to Mihi.

"What do you think they are up to?" Mihi asked.

"Wish I knew."

"What shall we do?"

"Well, it's a blessing that the weather is getting worse. I doubt anyone would be foolish enough to come ashore in a dinghy in this gale, so it's unlikely they will try anything tonight. Then again, we shouldn't assume anything. We'll need to do shifts through the night. I'll do the first four hours and you can do the next."

The weather was still miserable early next morning when Rick went to check on the harbour. Now four whale chasers were anchored there, one against the other like a club sandwich, and out in the bay, the mother ship, with two anchors out, was facing the incoming swell.

Through his binoculars Rick could see seamen assembling on the beach, some carrying guns, and others holding long poles with blades that looked like flensing knives used for cutting up the harpooned whales. It wasn't a good sign. He hurried back to tell Mihi.

Together they hunted through the cupboards for anything they could use to shelter under outside. They found two very large black polythene rubbish bags, which they stuffed into Rick's backpack before moving away from the approaching Japanese. Large areas of the island were covered with waist-high tussock and masses thorn-like bushes that had been prostrated by the prevailing winds. Rick felt the safest place for them would be as near to the Japanese boats as possible, in an area the Japanese would least expect to find them. So, taking great care not to leave any footprints, they doubled back down a seal and penguin track at the bottom of a shallow gully.

At what they considered to be a suitable site, they got down on their hands and knees and, pestered by myriads of flies, forced their way into a tangle of tussock and excavated a hollow in the cold, damp peaty soil beneath the grasses. Rick spread armfuls of tussock in the depression, and then cut open one of the rubbish bags and spread it out over the pile of grass. Wearing all their spare clothing, they lay on top of this, and covered themselves as best they could with the other opened bag as some protection from the cold drizzle. Rick then brushed the growing tussock back over them.

On and off through the day they heard Japanese voices calling. Occasionally they heard a whistle blow. Once, a couple of Japanese seamen came up the shallow gully in which they were hiding. The two men were talking casually and seemed to be on their way to join a search group further up the island. Being four hundred and sixty-five kilometres south of Aotearoa, the summer sun set very late, which made it a long and cramped day for Rick and Mihi. The cold swampy ground beneath them drained the heat from their bodies, not allowing them to relax.

"We are so well-hidden here," Mihi whispered to Rick, "that if we froze to death in an ice storm, we would never be found."

"I don't expect they will spend too much more time looking for us," said Rick. "Every day they are ashore means one less day hunting whales. I'm hoping if they don't find us soon, they will pack up and leave."

"On the other hand," added Mihi, "they know that if we escape and reveal what they are doing, this will probably be their last season." After sunset they edged cautiously out to stretch their legs and have something to eat. Rick insisted they eat their home-made cheese in order to fuel their inner furnaces. Then they returned to their nest to try to sleep through the hours of darkness, but they dozed fitfully, huddled together.

At the first glimmer of dawn Rick took his binoculars and went to a knob from which he could look down on the beach. He spent an hour lying on his belly in the tussock trying to work out, from the movements of the Japanese, what they intended to do. He watched the seamen gathering on the sand and noticed an almost hysterical officer running back and forth, continually jabbing his finger up in his direction. All heads turned to look. Rick knew they couldn't see him, so wondered what had got their attention.

It suddenly occurred to him that a flash of morning sunlight might have reflected off the lens of his binoculars. He was angry with himself for such carelessness. Suddenly there was a roar of triumphant voices as the seamen surged along the beach and began climbing up the slope towards him. With great care Rick eased himself down out of sight and raced back to Mihi. "I fear they've got our scent at last, sweetheart," he confessed. "I was a bit careless and I think they spotted me. Start praying, but for goodness' sake, pray silently."

Within a few minutes they could hear the approach of excited voices as a wall of seamen worked their way up the gully, through the matted ground cover, prodding every likely hiding place with the blades of their flensing knives. It seemed only a matter of minutes before they would be discovered.

Mihi mouthed the words of Psalm 34:17: *The righteous cry out, and the Lord hears them; He delivers them from all their troubles.* "Lord, we really need your help," she prayed. "Please, Lord, please! For our sakes, and the sakes of the folk back home in Aotearoa, please deliver us!"

No more than an occasional comment from the approaching seamen indicated the seriousness of their task. The swish of tussock grass on trouser legs as the searchers forced their way through it towards them could now be clearly heard. A searcher cleared his throat nearby, then, a moment later, a flensing knife sliced through the top of their cover and drove into the ground by Rick's right ear, opening up a large L-shaped tear to reveal Rick's face with his left forefinger pressed vertically against his pursed lips and a pistol in his right hand aimed at the chest of the man above him. The seaman on the other end of the lance froze, his eyes wide in shock. Their gazes locked.

Just when it seemed that either one or the other would give way under the mounting tension, three double blasts followed by a long one from the mother ship's horn down in the bay, reverberated in the still morning air. Before the echoes had died away, a rapid-speaking voice came across the water from the ship's loudspeaker. The searchers stopped and turned to listen. An officer about fifty metres back down the gully cried out something in staccato tones. The seamen, with the exception of the man standing over Rick, began to gather back onto the seal track and descend to the beach. Rick could feel his pulse throbbing in his temples as he stared up the gun barrel at the Japanese man's chest. The flood of adrenaline surging through his veins was now making his gun-hand shake.

The impatient Japanese officer down on the beach broke the tension by directing a stream of verbal abuse at the tardy seaman who was standing over them. While Rick and Mihi could not understand what the officer was saying, they could not mistake the insulting tone of his screeching voice. It wasn't nice. The offended man, with a sneer directed at his abusive officer, withdrew his lance with a jerk and sullenly turned to join the other seamen on their way back to the beach.

Rick and Mihi, shaking in reaction to the stress of their close encounter, didn't move for another hour and a half. When they finally came out of hiding there was no sign of the Japanese boats. Expelling a long breath through pursed lips Rick said, "That's what one would call a very, very close shave; no pun intended."

Mihi looked like someone who had just run a marathon. "Why, Lord, did you leave our rescue to the very last second?" she questioned with upturned eyes. Brushing dirt from her clothing she asked Rick, "Why do you think they left in such a hurry?"

"I have no idea. But one thing I do understand a lot better than I did before, is the meaning of the word providential."

"Do you think their departure might be a trick?" asked Mihi.

"What do you mean?" Rick replied.

"Perhaps the boats have gone to make us think that they have given up, but there could be observers stationed around the island waiting for us to come out of hiding. Once they spot us, they'll call the boats back."

"I hadn't thought of that possibility," replied Rick, looking about him. "I doubt it, though, because it doesn't explain why they gave up their hunt for us before they had finished searching the gully we were hiding in. Their leaving was just too abrupt. They didn't leave because they had run out of options, if you get what I mean."

"Even so, I think it would be a good idea to remain low until we are sure. Our patience must outlast theirs."

CHAPTER THIRTEEN

Forty minutes later, Rick cocked his head to one side. "Do you hear that?" he asked.

"Hear what?"

"It sounds like a ship's engine."

"I can't hear a thi . . . Yeeess. I can now! Do you think they are coming back?"

"No, this is a big ship. Sounds too sophisticated to be theirs. Turbines rather than pistons. Guess we'll find out soon enough."

A little later the high prow of a large white tourist cruise ship came around the headland.

"Wow!" exclaimed Mihi. "What a beautiful boat!"

"It's the Antarctica Princess," said Rick from behind his binoculars. "If I remember correctly, it is a cruise ship that does what they call the Lower Pacific Circle. It starts its journey starts in Brisbane, comes south down the Great Barrier Reef to Sydney, then to some sub-Antarctic Islands, across the Antarctic Continent, and then up to Puerto Montt and Valparaiso in Chile."

After a few moments Rick added, "I bet that's why the Japanese whalers took off in a hurry. The cruise ship can only stop here if it has an officer on board from the Australian Parks and Wildlife Service. It would be bad enough for Japanese whalers to be caught in the South Pacific Whale Sanctuary, but to be also found illegally on an Australian Reserve without a permit would create a double-whammy international incident."

"This is not an Australian Reserve, Ricky! The Auckland Islands belong to Aotearoa!"

"Yeah, I know. But the Australians took them over after the epidemic because they didn't want the Japanese or anyone else moving in," Rick reminded her.

The liner anchored in the bay between Rose and Ocean Islands. A large covered motorboat was lowered over the side and passengers stepped into the boat from a door in the side of the ship and were then motored to a point further up the bay.

"We need to make some smoke to get their attention," said Mihi.

Gathering armfuls of semi-dry tussock, they made several failed attempts before eventually getting it to light. Once it was burning fiercely, they piled on more tussock until clouds of white smoke rose high above them. The fire had been going for five or six minutes before they noticed a smaller motorboat coming in their direction.

Rick and Mihi raced down to the beach.

"I'm hardly in any state to meet anyone," said Mihi. "And you, with your whiskers, look like the wild man from Borneo."

The first person to clamber from the boat was a uniformed Parks and Wildlife officer. His initial shock at seeing Mihi carrying a gun turned to belligerence. "Who the hell are you?" he demanded. "And what are you doing with a gun in a protected wildlife area?"

Mihi was tempted to reply, "This island belongs to us, not to you Australians. What right have you got to be here?" but she thought better of it.

Rick responded, "We're castaways, trying to get home to Australia. We've lost our boat and need your help."

"What was the name of your boat?" he snapped.

"The *SpinDrift*. From Port Douglas."

"Hmmm," the officer replied, stroking his chin. "I remember that. But that was last Easter, almost a year ago."

"That's right," affirmed Rick, offering no further information to enlighten the officer.

"Look, I have no authority to invite you onboard the Antarctic Princess. I'll have to talk to the … *Ooahh!*" he cried, screwing up his face and arching his back in pain before doubling up with one hand pressed against his abdomen.

Mihi rushed to his side and held his upper arm with both hands. "Are you alright? What's wrong?"

The officer remained bent over for about a minute, unable to speak. His breathing was laboured and Mihi noticed he was sweating profusely. On hearing his cry, a crewman came running up the beach. "This is not the first attack he has had," he explained. "I told him he needed to see the ship's doctor."

Eventually the pain subsided, and the officer stood and wiped beads of cold sweat from his brow. Taking a deep breath he said, "Excuse me a moment." His back was arched, as though seeking to assuage some internal agony, but he hobbled slowly away from them, unclipping a radio from his belt as he went. After a mumbled conversation he returned and asked, "What are your names?

"My name is Rick Carter, and this is my wife, Mihi."

"Their names are Rick and May Carter," he said into his R.T. "—husband and wife. Okay, I'll bring them back to the ship."

"Mr Carter," the officer said, "the captain has given you permission to go on board." Then pointing to Mihi's gun he added, "But you won't be allowed on board with that!" Rick shrugged his shoulders, took the gun by the barrel and flung it out into the sea. Once he was in the launch, he discretely dropped their pistol over the side.

On the ship, Rick and Mihi were met by a steward and taken to a vacant cabin. They were told they had five hours to bathe and get cleaned up, and that the captain had requested the pleasure of having them dine with him at his own table at seven that evening.

"The only clothes that we have are the ones we're standing up in," Mihi said. "As you can see, they are in no condition to be worn into the ship's dining room."

"They are nice clothes, just a little soiled," commented the steward. "After you have showered, put on the bathrobes in your cabin and give me a call. I'll collect your clothes and have them dry cleaned, pressed, and returned to you within an hour. By the way, there are drinks and snacks in the refrigerator."

"What are all these knobs for?" Mihi asked as she climbed into the spacious hot tub with Rick.

"Sit down and I'll show you," Rick replied.

"Whee!" she squealed as jets of bubbles foamed up around her. "This is wonderful."

They luxuriated in bath gels, shampoos and conditioners, and lay back with wine glasses filled with sweet sparkling white grape juice from Spain as their body temperatures slowly returned to normal.

"I need a haircut," said Mihi as she towelled herself dry.

"Let's ask the steward when he comes for our clothes," Rick suggested.

The steward told them they could use their cabin phone to order a cut, and, with Rick's help, Mihi made the call. The voice on the other end said, "We can take you now, as most of the tourists have gone ashore. Would you like to come to our salon, or would you prefer us to come to you?"

"Please come to us," Mihi said confidently.

Within minutes a male hairdresser arrived at their door with a cart of accessories and equipment. "Oh, my goodness! You have such beautiful hair," he enthused in a Greek accent. "I'd really like to do something with it. May I use your television please?"

He pressed a button on the remote and spoke a single word: "Hairdresser." A display came up on the wall screen. "This is what I have in mind for you," he said, zeroing in on a hairstyle. "It suits your face and hair perfectly. When I have finished with you, you will be so proud you will stand a few centimetres taller."

"Thank you," said Mihi. "Do you mind if I look at the other styles?"

"Please do."

Eventually she agreed that he had made the right choice for her and submitted her head to his scissors.

As the hairdresser snipped at her length of hair, Mihi asked, "Where do the tourists on this boat come from? From my observation most of them are older people."

"Ah yes, but not all. They come from all over the world. There are many languages spoken on this ship, Greek being just one of them. There is also a large contingent of media moguls on board. They are mixing business with pleasure, so to speak. While the ship is sailing, they hold their conference, and when we are in port or sailing along the Antarctic coast, they do sight-seeing. Very nice if you can afford it. By the way, how will you pay for this service? With cash or by credit card?"

Rick, who had noticed the satellite television and was catching up on the ABC News spoke up, "I need to make a visit to the purser. Have you any idea what hours he keeps?"

"Yes, he will be open in a few minutes for two hours."

"Good. As soon as my clothes come back from the cleaners I'll go and see him and get some cash to pay you."

When the hairdresser had finished cutting, he said, "Now we are going to give you a perm which will turn your hair in at the base. I just need to the rollers in position. And while the perm is being fixed, I think I should give you a haircut and a shave, Mr. Carter, don't you think?"

"Yeah, not a bad idea," said Rick fingering the hair at the back of his head. "I'd really appreciate that."

While his hair was being trimmed the doorbell rang and the hairdresser was given a neatly folded stack of laundered clothing for Rick and Mihi. Rick, dressed and coiffured, admired himself in the full-length mirror, then slapped some aftershave around his neck before setting out to find the purser's office. He carried with him a small canvas bag containing six gold ingots.

"I'm Rick Carter, Cabin 401," said Rick.

The purser repeated, "Rick Carter, room 401," to his computer. Scanning the screen he said, "I'm afraid I don't have you listed, Mr. Carter. And according to my records Cabin 401 is empty."

"That was correct until a couple of hours ago. We have just come aboard."

The purser raised an eyebrow: "From the Auckland Islands?"

"Yes, from the Auckland Islands."

"This is highly unusual. Can't say we have ever taken passengers on board from the Auckland Islands before. Is the captain aware of your presence on board?"

"He has invited my wife and I to have dinner with him this evening."

"Oh," he replied with pursed lips. "I see. And what can I do for you."

"I need some money. US dollars."

"And how much would you like?"

"This much," said Rick, placing the canvas bag on the counter.

The purser loosened the tie and shook out the contents.

"Are these what I think they are, Mr. Carter?" he asked, picking one up and swivelling around to examine it under a desk light.

"Yep!" replied Rick.

"May I ask where you got them from?"

"No! You may not. But they do belong to me, and they were obtained honestly."

"Mr. Carter, this is one of the more unusual transactions that have come across this desk, and it may not come as a surprise to you that we don't have the figures on the latest gold prices. Furthermore, I may have to wait until the next transmission to get them. Let me weigh them in your presence and I'll give you a receipt for them. If you are in need of urgent cash, I would be willing to give you an advance of two thousand US dollars."

"That would suit me fine, thank you," said Rick, not believing how easy the transaction had been.

"Do you have a cash card that I can credit the money to?"

"I'm sorry. I don't."

"Would you like me to issue you with one?"

"Please."

Back in the cabin the hairdresser was packing up. Rick thanked and paid him, then shut the door behind him before looking up and gasping. Mihi had come out of the bedroom wearing her hand-tooled waistcoat and a fine leather skirt that fell below her knees. She looked absolutely stunning. Rick just stood there and gawked at her.

She broke the spell. "Ricky, darling, we both need new footwear. I noticed that what we are wearing is very different from what other people on this boat are wearing."

"Ship."

"Ship?"

"Yes, this is a ship, not a boat."

"What's the difference?"

"You can put a boat on a ship, but not the other way round."

"Okay. But we need new shoes."

"It seems that we can track down most things over the phone so let's give it a go," suggested Rick. "Here's something that looks promising."

Rick spoke with someone, then told Mihi that the shoe shop was in the process of closing for the day but would stay open for them if they went right away. Within minutes, Rick had purchased a nice pair of light tan suede shoes while Mihi chose some lovely strapped shoes with a medium heel. It was the first time she had ever owned anything like them, and she felt and looked absolutely feminine with them on her feet.

Turning to Rick, she said, "Ricky, there's something I especially want to do, but we need to go back to the cabin."

Looking into her eyes, Ricky could see that she was very serious. "Okay. We've still got an hour before dinner," he agreed. "Let's go."

Back in the cabin Mihi locked the door and switched off the phone. "Ricky, darling, I have a great peace inside me that we are safe at last. I know it won't be over until we can secure the peace and safety of our people in Aotearoa, but I believe that the main battle has been won. We owe such a huge debt of gratitude to God and I want to thank him for bringing us through safely. I am still astounded by his providential leading over the last few weeks."

"Yes," replied Rick thoughtfully. "It's unbelievable. Several times I thought the end had come, but it wasn't the end of the story— just another chapter."

"There's one other thing, too, that I want us to thank God for. I believe I'm pregnant."

Rick gawked at her with his mouth open, stuck for words. "Oh Mihi. What wonderful news," he cried, falling to his knees. "Thank you, Thank you, God! Lord, how can I thank you enough for all these blessings? There's just so many of them. Thank you for bringing Mihi into my life. What a precious, precious wife she is to me. So gentle, so loving, so patient, so strong and so beautiful. She's a woman of integrity. Through her I have come to know you, Jesus, as my Lord and Saviour. And thank you, Holy Spirit, my guide, teacher, protector and comforter. Thank you, Father, for caring for us, your children."

Placing his hand on Mihi's belly he continued, "And I especially thank you for this new life that's forming inside Mihi. I ask only that this child will be a true reflection of its mother. Thank you, Lord, for this precious, precious gift."

Then Mihi broke in, "Lord, I want to thank you for Ricky. He is a wonderful man who is open to you, and he loves and cares for me. I love him so very, very much. We thank you for bringing us safely to this ship. We realise that it's not over yet, but we believe the end is in sight, at long last. Lord, we want to commit the rest of our trip into your care, praying that you will help to make our cause known to the free world. And, please, God, bless our families back home, especially J.B., Carla, Cardiac and Ari's families who are still grieving the loss of their loved ones. And Lord, there's just one other thing . . ." She began to sniff. "Please, please forgive me for shooting that Australian soldier."

At this she broke down in tears. Rick reached out and drew her to his side. Through her sobs she continued, "Please comfort the family of that poor young man. Send good people to support them in their loss. Amen."

They stood and Rick held her close. After a while Mihi said, "I need to wash my face."

As she was patting her cheeks and eyes dry Rick said, "We've been through some rough times, sweetheart, but I have to say that I have never ever been so at peace in my life. Being safe on this ship with my wife and future child is, for me, a foretaste of the kingdom of heaven."

At the Captain's table the steward seated them behind their name cards, Rick and May Carter. Two other couples joined them, and when Captain Burton-Smith arrived, they all stood. He waved them back down. "Please be seated. Now, let me see. I think it would be best if we began with introductions all around. Please tell us who you are and what you do. We'll start with our newest passengers, Mr and Mrs Carter."

Rick began, "I'm Rick Carter. I'm a primary school teacher from Port Douglas in Australia, and I'm on leave of absence."

Captain Burton-Smith leaned across the table. "Tell me, Rick, what kind of work were you and Mrs. Carter engaged in, down here on the Auckland Islands, when you lost your boat? Were you involved in some flora or fauna research?"

"No, nothing like that. We are here purely by chance," Rick replied. "Or providence. We got to the Auckland Islands by a round-a-bout way—too long a story to share over one meal."

"I see. And what about you, Mrs. Carter? Tell us about yourself."

"My name is Mihi, which means greeting." Picking up their name card she said, "The first name given me here is a mistake. And, I'm from Aotearoa."

"New Zealand?" asked the captain.

"Yes."

"Your parents or grandparents were from New Zealand?" he added.

"No. I was born in Aotearoa and lived there all my life until a few weeks ago. I met Rick there and we were married in Auckland recently."

"You're pulling our legs, of course," laughed one of the other guests.

"No, I'm not!" said Mihi innocently. "Why do you think I have come to the table tonight dressed in hand-tooled leather clothing while all the other ladies are in smart suits. It's because this is the type of clothing we wear in Aotearoa. I have nothing else."

There was a stunned silence. Then Mrs. Kingsford-Allen spoke up. "But how can you come from New Zealand when there's nobody left alive there?"

"I'm not sure where you got the impression that there are no people living in Aotearoa," replied Mihi. "I know of three separate populations in the North Island, and they are all viable and healthy."

"Excuse me for butting in," said Rick, "but may we have the rest of the introductions before we continue. It would be nice to know who we are talking to."

"This is absolutely incredible," said Mrs. Kingsford-Allen in an aside to her husband as she nervously moved her chair out and in and out again.

"Yes. Forgive me," said the captain. "Mr. and Mrs Marchant, would you be so kind as to introduce yourselves next?"

Mr. Marchant hooked his finger over his bowtie and coughed. "This is quite extraordinary," he muttered to no one in particular. Then bringing himself to order he said, "Ah yes. I'm Ulysses Marchant. I spend most of my year in Los Angeles. I'm the owner of the All-American Digital TV Network. That takes all my time. This is the first break for leisure that I've had in two years."

"I'm MariJayne Marchant," his wife continued. "It's my job to maintain the peace, keep my husband sane, and help spend his money."

"And I'm Compton Kingsford-Allen," said the next person holding up his name card between his thumb and forefinger. "Like Ulysses here, I also come from the United States, except I live in New York on the East Coast. My wife and I change hemispheres according to the weather, migrating to Sydney during the northern winter. My vocation? Yes, I've just sold up my shares in computer software and have purchased the World-wide Network News Company, *UniTell*. We're on this ship for the same conference-cum-holiday." Everyone at the table then looked at his wife.

"I'm Marguerite Kingsford-Allen. As you can see, I'm quite a bit younger than my husband and am, therefore, not yet content to sit at home. I have a key role in the new company as a manager. You'd be bored with the details. Now I'm impatient to be getting back to this Aotea-what's-it's-name story."

"Aotearoa," corrected Mihi nicely.

"Yes. Yes. I'm dying to hear more." Then looking closely at Mihi she asked, "Your story is quite unbelievable. You haven't been popping drugs have you, darling?"

"My wife won't even drink alcohol!" Rick retorted. Then in a change of tone he added, "I'll tell you how you can check out our story. And it can be done quite easily from this ship. Just get in contact with the Queensland Coastguard Station at Coolangatta and ask them to check their records for Rick Carter last Easter. My yacht, the *SpinDrift*, was blown down the Tasman by Cyclone Funi. It foundered on a sandbank at the Manukau Heads. If it wasn't for Mihi and her people, I wouldn't be here today."

The captain interrupted. "Excuse me, please, Mr Carter." Then addressing everyone he continued, "Tonight we are having a smorgasbord, so I suggest we break off this conversation until we have filled our plates."

Back at the table, Marguerite Kingsford-Allen once again led the questioning. "I find your story hard to believe. If there are people living in New Zealand, why hasn't the rest of the world heard about them? We heard that the Indonesians tried to colonise the country several years back, but that they were totally wiped out by the Leoenzide plague. How come you survived but they didn't?" Then, looking at her plate she said, "I hate olives. How did I manage to pick up olives? You didn't put them there, did you, Comp?"

Rick tapped the rim of his plate with a knife. "I'll tell you what I will do for you," he said. "Because you are still sceptical about our story, we'll offer you some additional evidence which you can check out. During the ten months that I was in New Zealand I met a number of Australian servicemen, both soldiers and sailors, who were on duty there."

Hearing this, Marchant and Kingsford-Allen glanced at each other with expressionless faces. "Their mission to New Zealand is top-secret, so they would get into serious trouble if it were reported that they had even been to the country. I believe that I could give you the names of about ten of them, including one who was killed on service there. You men, with all your contacts, could check them out discretely. That should be enough to convince you that we are telling the truth."

Mr. Kingsford-Allen leaned across the table. "I'd like to take you up on your offer. Here's my notebook and a pen. Give me as many facts as you can about these men: their names and the branch of the military that they are, or were, in. If this story is true, it rates in my mind as the story of the decade. This is big news indeed, wouldn't you agree, Compton?"

"I'm utterly astonished. We had no inkling there were people living in New Zealand."

Rick took the pen and, conferring with Mihi, they were able to recall nine surnames, the ranks of most of them, and the service that they were in. He also gave him Draper's and Carson's names and the dates on which they died.

"Thank you," said Kingsford-Allen as he tucked his notebook back into his pocket. "My wife and I would like to invite you to have dinner with us tomorrow night. Unless, of course, you both want to go ashore to watch the yellow-eyed penguins come in at dusk."

"We have already spent one night ashore with penguins and seals, and that was more than sufficient," said Mihi. "Yes, we'd be delighted to dine with you."

"Are we in on that dinner deal?" asked Marchant.

"Of course," said Kingsford-Allen. Then turning to Rick, he said, "We'll call for you at six-forty-five in the evening tomorrow."

The next day Rick took Mihi for a tour of the Antarctica Princess. Mihi was awed by the opulence but not at all impressed by the superficiality of many people. She loved the chamber orchestra but couldn't get out of the casino quick enough. She was impressed by the array of equipment in the gymnasium, and enjoyed the sauna and swim, but was disgusted by the small talk and the petty criticisms of the people she met. "People who feel that they have to tear others down in order to make themselves look good must be very shallow."

"One place I'd love to see," added Mihi, "is the ship's engine room."

Rick sucked a stream of air through his teeth. "I don't know that they allow passengers down into the engine room, but we can ask." They asked a steward who directed them to the chief engineer.

"It's not normal practice to show passengers around the engine room," the chief said. Then with a smile added, "But for you I think we could make an exception. Follow me." Over his shoulder he said, "We wouldn't be able to show you around while under way, but here at anchor it should be no problem."

Down below, the temperature was quite tropical. After seeing the stabilisers that helped keep the ship on an even keel in rough weather, and the great turbines that drove the propellers, Mihi said, "I'm very impressed with how clean and neat everything is down here. You could eat your food off this machinery."

The officer couldn't contain a grin, and his chest visibly swelled. "Aren't you the New Zealand couple who've just come aboard?" he asked.

"I'm a Kiwi," corrected Mihi. "Ricky's an Aussie."

"The whole ship is abuzz about you two. The radio officer told me that bookings have been placed for thirty-nine ship-to-shore calls tomorrow evening. Apparently it's got something to do with an address that you will be giving."

"News to me," said Rick with a shrug of his shoulders.

Back on deck, Mihi turned to Rick and asked, "What did you make of that?"

"I have no idea," he replied. "I'm as much in the dark as you are. Here comes Mr. Kingsford-Allen. Perhaps he can enlighten us."

Compton Kingsford-Allen puffed up to them. "Been looking all over for you two. I've done some checking. You were confirmed missing after Cyclone Funi. I also checked out those names that you gave me and they all ring true except for Thomas Draper. He was listed as missing back in 2025. Yet you say he died this year."

"That's right," said Rick. "He came to New Zealand several years ago but because of his crime was condemned to exile in the Coromandel Peninsula. He lived there until his death this year."

"Very interesting! This case is becoming more and more intriguing," Compton replied.

"Did your research uncover the reason for Carson's death?" asked Rick.

"It was reported that he died of internal injuries due to a fall down the flight deck lift-well on an aircraft carrier while stationed in the Tasman."

Rick and Mihi looked at each other but their expressions gave nothing away.

"Look," said Kingsford-Allen, "I need to duck off to arrange something. We'll see you both at dinner tonight."

"Let's go to the purser's office," said Rick. "He should have something for us."

The purser asked Rick to sign a couple of forms, after which he deposited a healthy sum on Rick's cash card. As they walked away, Mihi squeezed Rick's arm. "Finally, we'll be able to buy ourselves some nice clothes," she laughed.

Right on six-forty-five that evening, the doorbell rang and a steward invited Rick and Mihi to follow him to a private dining room. Inside they found the Kingsford-Allens and the Marchants. With them was one other person in Australian military uniform. Kingsford-Allen introduced him as Colonel Petersen. Colonel Petersen stood and shook hands with Rick and Mihi. Although they both had an inbuilt suspicion of Australian soldiers, Rick immediately warmed to Petersen. As they pulled their chairs in to the table and sat down, the Colonel said, "I'm very interested to hear what you have to say about New Zealand."

Rick immediately responded: "Inasmuch as our report will run counter to the propaganda issued by the Australian Government, why would you—a man who is committed to upholding the Government's policies—want to hear something that would create a cognitive dissonance for you?"

"I want to assure you, Mr. Carter, that you will not be creating any cognitive dissonance, as you call it, by sharing with us the truth about the people of New Zealand. That already exists. After every mission to New Zealand, we are faced with facts in our debriefings that just don't fit the standard government line. Several top military personnel who have been sent to New Zealand have resigned rather than return there. When interviewed off-camera they tell us that conditions in New Zealand are not what they have been led to believe. That's why I want to hear what you have to say."

Mihi, who had been sitting very still and quiet, began to sob. Rick leaned over, put his hand on hers and whispered, "What's the matter, sweetheart?"

She stood up and turned to face the officer. With tears streaming down her cheeks she said, "Please forgive my unrestrained emotion, but I'm finding it very difficult to be in the same room as a senior officer of the armed forces that tried to exterminate us Kiwis as if we were noxious pests. All we wanted to do in Aotearoa is live at peace, and you have sent your forces over to napalm and bomb us, and shoot us like rabbits. And you have forced us to defend ourselves with guns. You may not be aware of the fact that just a few weeks ago I had to shoot and kill one of your soldiers to prevent him from killing others. I hate myself for having done that, and will carry that burden for the rest of my life. You forced that upon us. Why do you persist in invading our land? Why can't you just leave us alone to live in peace?"

At this, Mihi sat down, buried her face in her hands and sobbed loudly. Rick drew her to him in an embrace, and there was an embarrassed silence as the others played with their table napkins. Eventually, MariJayne Marchant stood and said to Mihi, "Let me take you back to our cabin and leave the others to talk by themselves. I've got some Swiss chocolates there that I think you'd love."

Mihi looked at Rick, who nodded. As the two women turned and left, Compton Kingsford-Allen broke the tension. "Once again, food has become a secondary consideration," he remarked. "We'll fill our plates and talk while we eat, shall we?"

When everyone was seated again, the military officer turned to Rick and said with furrowed brow, "I think your wife was mistaken about shooting an Australian soldier. No Australian soldier has been shot in New Zealand."

"Sir, I was there when it happened. He was shot in the chest by Mihi just after he had gunned down one of our people in cold blood."

"Who was this soldier, Mr. Carter?"

"His name was Carson," Rick replied.

"Yes. Carson died, but not by a bullet, Mr. Carter," said the officer. "He died of internal injuries after a fall on the Aircraft Carrier, *ANV Pelican.*"

"Sir, I assure you that Carson did not die by a fall!" retorted Rick emphatically. "He was shot. I was there! I saw it happen with my own eyes. Have you seen his corpse? No! You haven't! Well, I helped wrap his body in canvas so that it would be protected from wild carnivores. If he hasn't been cremated, have him exhumed and check for yourself whether or not I'm telling the truth."

"Sounds to me like there has been some fudging of the truth by your branch of the forces, Colonel," commented Ulysses Marchant.

"Yes," he admitted. "If what Mr. Carter says is true—and it's my belief now that it has to be, for how else would he know about Carson's death? —it makes me wonder how many other lies have been told to us about events in New Zealand?"

"Which brings me to the reason why I invited you and your good lady to this meal, Mr. Carter," said Marchant. "As you know, there is a large contingent of media professionals here on the Antarctica Princess. Part of our package tour was to be three evening lectures by the Parks and Wildlife Service officer who is travelling with us.

But unfortunately—or fortunately, depending on one's perspective—he is indisposed due to an attack of kidney stones. The poor man is in severe pain in the ship's hospital and is heavily sedated. Compton and I, who organised this media trip, are wondering if you would mind sharing with us the story of your New Zealand adventure over three evenings. I'm afraid you won't have too much time to prepare, as the first lecture is due to start after dinner tomorrow."

The invitation left Rick mentally stunned. When he hesitated, Ulysses added, "Of course, there will be a fee. Or, if you prefer, we will cover the cost of the voyage for you and your wife. What do you say? Is it a goer?"

Rick smiled. "I'd be honoured."

There was clapping and mutters of 'wonderful' all around.

Rick then leaned over to Marchant and asked quietly, "What day is it today?"

"Wednesday," Marchant replied.

"Are you expecting me to give these three lectures on three consecutive evenings—Thursday, Friday, Saturday?"

"Normally we'd be happy to spread them over a week or so, but this is a very hot topic, Rick. After each lecture there will be transmissions to a world that will be waiting with bated breath for the next edition. I think it would be best if we had the lectures on three consecutive days."

"I'll be happy to start the lectures tomorrow night," replied Rick, "but I won't be available on Saturday night. The sun doesn't set till late in this latitude at this time of the year, and Saturday is my Sabbath. Of course, I'd be delighted to give the final lecture on Sunday, if that is alright with you."

"I'm sorry," apologised Marchant who looked disappointed. "We didn't know you were Jewish."

"I'm not," responded Rick. "I'm a Christian."

"But didn't you say Saturday?"

"Yes. Saturday is the biblical Sabbath. It's the day that Mihi and I observe as our rest day."

"Look, I don't understand why you are a Saturday Christian and not a Sunday Christian, but giving a lecture hardly falls into the category of work. I'm sure it would be okay just to come along and tell us your story."

"Let me assure you, sir, that I would not be at peace if I did. I need to spend that day with the Lord and my wife. I hope you understand. Besides," Rick added with a smile, "a wait will only serve to whet everyone's appetite."

After the meal, Marchant told Kingsford-Allen about Rick's refusal to speak to them on Saturday evening. When Kingsford-Allen responded by saying that this seemed to provide them with a marvellous opportunity to do an article on Rick and Mihi Carter and their religious beliefs, Marchant raised his eyebrows and said, "Why didn't I think of that?"

That evening as Rick and Mihi lay in the spa pool together, Rick mused, "Aotearoa seems so far away, it's like a dream world."

"This is the dream world, Ricky."

"I wish the Waitak folk could see us now. They'd say, "What hath God wrought?"

"Yes. God has been good to us. But it's not over yet. We still need their prayers. Your three presentations are crucial. And so are the reports that will be radioed out to the world afterwards."

"You know something? As much as I enjoy this luxury, it's very superficial. I can't wait until I get back to good old Aotearoa. I love that place . . . and those people."

"Me too! Come here, you beautiful Maori woman."

"If you want me, you've got to catch me," Mihi challenged with a gleam in her eye.

CHAPTER FOURTEEN

The next evening Rick and Mihi, in their smart new outfits, were introduced by Kingsford-Allen to a theatre-full of media moguls. The lights were turned down and with two spotlights shining on them and the movie cameras rolling.

Rick began. ". . . Exhausted to the point of physical and mental numbness, I dragged myself from the pounding surf on my hands and knees and collapsed face down in a line of spume and rotting seaweed. I was safe at last. Or so I thought. For three unremitting days and nights I had battled the Easter Cyclone that drove my yacht down into the Tasman Sea. At the point of giving up, my yacht, *SpinDrift,* grounded on a sandbank near the Manukau Heads. Deciding that the time had come for me to part company with my boat, I unclipped my safety line and let the ocean rollers carry me ashore until I landed in a small bay at Whatipu. I was relieved be on solid ground, even if it was New Zealand . . ."